My Mom Married the Principal

Also by Margaret Bechard

Star Hatchling
Really No Big Deal
Tory and Me and the Spirit of True Love
My Sister, My Science Report

My Mom Married the Principal

Margaret Bechard

Viking

VIKING
Published by the Penguin Group
Penguin Putnam Inc., 375 Hudson Street, New York, New York 10014, U.S.A.
Penguin Books Ltd, 27 Wrights Lane, London W8 5TZ, England
Penguin Books Australia Ltd, Ringwood, Victoria, Australia
Penguin Books Canada Ltd, 10 Alcorn Avenue, Toronto, Ontario, Canada M4V 3B2
Penguin Books (N.Z.) Ltd, 182-190 Wairau Road, Auckland 10, New Zealand
Penguin Books Ltd, Registered Offices: Harmondsworth, Middlesex, England

First published in 1998 by Viking, a member of Penguin Putnam Inc.

3 5 7 9 10 8 6 4 2

LIBRARY OF CONGRESS CATALOGING-IN-PUBLICATION DATA
Bechard, Margaret.
My mom married the principal / by Margaret Bechard.
p.   cm.
Summary: Eighth-grader Jonah Truman's life gets more complicated after his mom
marries his school's principal during summer vacation.
ISBN 0-670-87394-2 (hardcover)
[1. Schools—Fiction.   2. Stepfamilies—Fiction.   3. Friendship—Fiction.]
I. Title.
PZ7.B380655Mo   1998   [Fic]—dc21   97-22653   CIP   AC

Printed in U.S.A.
Set in Melior

To Deborah Brodie, with thanks for your editorial wisdom and patience. It was all your idea.

Contents

Still Plain Old Jonah Truman

Travis Hunter and Tiffany Finley were kissing in front of the drinking fountain. I knew because I was watching them around the open door of my locker.

"Jonah!"

Emma Hardy and Sylvie Tompkins pushed their way through the crowd of kids milling around before first period.

"How's it going?" I turned and pretended I'd been looking for something in my locker.

Emma had spotted Travis and Tiffany. She nudged Sylvie. "How long's that been going on?"

About five minutes, I thought.

"Since Monday," Sylvie said. "Tiffany dumped Gordon on Friday during English."

"Wow. And now it's Thursday, and Tiffany and Travis

1

are *still* together? A world record." Emma looked at me. "Hey, Jonah. I have a really important question to ask you."

I didn't know Emma or Sylvie real well, but I did know Emma could be sort of goofy. "What's the question?"

Emma wagged a finger at me. "Why does your nose run, but your feet smell?"

For just a second, I thought she was serious. Because she looked really serious and because, actually, my feet did sort of smell. But then she burst out laughing. "I mean, isn't it bizarre? Your feet should run, and your nose should smell."

I thought it was sort of dumb, but I laughed, too. Emma had that kind of laugh. "You're right," I said. "It's weird."

They had stopped kissing, and now Travis was playing with the zipper on Tiffany's jacket.

"It's not weird," Sylvie said. "It's dumb." She shoved in between Emma and me. "I have a *really* important question."

Emma made a face, and I laughed again.

Sylvie frowned at me. "Is it true your mom got married to the principal over the summer?"

I stopped laughing. It was the third week of school. You'd think this would be old news by now. "It's true," I said.

"Is your name Jonah Decker now?" Emma asked.

"No. I'm still Jonah Truman." Good old, plain old, boring old Jonah Truman.

"Do you call him Bob or Mr. Decker?" Emma asked.

"Bob."

She nodded. "I call my stepfather Phil. But I call my stepmom Mom." She sighed. "It's a long story."

Sylvie shifted her binder to her other arm. "Do you mind?" She gave Emma a dirty look. "The thing is, Jonah. Seeing as how you know Mr. Decker so well? I was wondering if you could get me transferred out of Spurl's class."

"Mr. Spurl will make you hurl," Emma said.

"It's not that," Sylvie said. "I have to get into Conway's class. With Evan Gillespie."

"She's thinking about asking him to go out with her," Emma said, and Sylvie smiled and nodded.

I sighed. Everybody in the entire eighth grade was going out with somebody, or about to ask somebody to go out. Everybody but me. "Sylvie," I said. "*I* am in Spurl's class."

"So?"

"So, if I could get anybody out of there, don't you think I'd get me out?" My voice went up, and a group of sixth graders veered around us, staring and giggling.

3

Sylvie frowned. "You don't have to get mad about it."

"She was just asking, Jonah," Emma said.

"I'm not mad about it."

"I thought you said he was a nice guy." Sylvie turned toward Emma, like I'd disappeared into thin air.

"He used to be a very nice guy." They both walked away, shaking their heads.

"I *am* a nice guy," I said.

"Sure you are." Kevin Martinez had come up behind me. "What was that all about?"

"A Bob favor."

Kevin laughed. He pulled open his locker next to mine. "How many is that? Four?"

"Five. Jake stopped me after P.E. yesterday and asked if I could get him into a Spanish class with better-looking girls."

Kevin looked thoughtful. "Now that's a good idea."

I slammed my locker shut. "Not you, too," I said. I leaned my head against the door and groaned. The sound echoed out of the little vent. I laughed. "Hey, Kev. Listen to this." I did it again.

"Cool." Kevin put his mouth up to his vent and burped.

"*What* are you guys doing?" Amanda Matzinger was standing behind us. Katherine Chang was with her. My face started to burn.

4

"Sylvie asked Jonah for a Bob favor," Kevin said. He didn't even sound embarrassed.

"And that makes you burp?" Amanda gave Kevin a shove, and he shoved her back, and they did a little pushing and shoving thing across the hall. Amanda and Kevin had been going out since last spring, and they were always shoving and pushing each other.

Katherine was smiling at me. I smiled back. This was it. This was my chance to say something nice to Katherine Chang. To maybe even ask her to go out with me. I opened my mouth. I could hear the words loud and clear in my head. But I couldn't actually say them. I opened my mouth wider.

Katherine frowned. "Are you okay?"

I nodded. I closed my mouth and took a deep breath.

Amanda and Kevin had shoved back to our side of the hall. Amanda looked at Travis and Tiffany. They were kissing again. "He is such a jerk," Amanda said.

"What does she see in him?" Katherine asked.

The door across the hall opened, and Bob walked out. He was wearing the tie Mom had gotten him for his birthday and a sort of hairy-looking sweater. He spotted Travis and Tiffany right away. "No overt displays of affection in the hallways," he said loudly.

They leapt apart. Tiffany turned around and started getting a drink. "I was just waiting in line for the drinking fountain," Travis said. "My mouth gets really dry in the mornings." Tiffany started giggling, and water spurted out of her mouth.

"You'd better get moving, people," Bob said. "You're going to be late." He glanced up and down the hallway. He looked right past me, like he didn't even know me, which I thought was sort of nice of him.

"We'd better go," Katherine said. "We don't want to be late for science."

Mrs. Manning always started class by reading the announcements. She had the kind of adult voice that was easy to space out. I looked over at Katherine. Because we had to sit in alphabetical order, she was way on the other side of the room, by the windows. If I *had* changed my name to Decker, I'd be sitting right behind her. And maybe if I were sitting behind her, I'd work up the nerve to ask her to go out with me.

A Pink Pearl eraser hit me, hard, on the side of the head and bounced onto my desk. Two rows over, Emma was looking up at the ceiling, pretending to whistle.

I waited until Mrs. Manning started handing out

weather charts. Then I lobbed the eraser back at Emma. Only I missed. The eraser hit Travis, behind her, instead.

"Hey!" Travis shouted. "Hey! Somebody hit me with an eraser!"

"Oh, my gosh, Travis," Emma said. "It would be more surprising if somebody *hadn't* hit you with an eraser."

Travis made a face, and the whole class started laughing, even Mrs. Manning. Emma grinned and gave me a thumbs-up. Mrs. Manning asked a question about cold fronts, and Katherine raised her hand to answer it.

Amanda stopped by my desk when class was over. "Katherine said she likes your hair like that."

"Really?" I checked, but Katherine was already gone. "When did she say that?"

"During that group activity thing. She said you looked really cute today. She likes your T-shirt, too." Amanda grinned. "I told her she should have seen you in first grade. Remember that Cookie Monster shirt you always wore?"

Not only does Amanda live next door to me, we've been in school together since preschool. She knows more embarrassing things about me than my mother. "Amanda." I stood up. "You don't have to tell her *everything* about me."

She poked me in the chest. "Face it, Jonah. You need all the help you can get."

On my way to social studies, I stopped in the bathroom to check my hair. It did look pretty good. Somehow I'd gotten it to lie down just right. I dug out my comb and smoothed the top. I'd have to remember to ask Mom to get some more dandruff shampoo. And some more zit cream. I leaned forward and checked the one on my chin. The late bell rang.

I was almost at the social studies classroom when Travis and his jerk buddy, Jerry Fitzner, caught up with me. They were laughing about something. "Jonah!" Travis dropped his arm across my shoulder.

"Hey, Travis," I said. Travis had started being nice to me last spring. I didn't know how long it was going to last.

"Good to see you, Jonah," Jerry said. He opened the classroom door, and I followed the two of them inside.

"You're late, gentlemen." Mr. Spurl sounded really mad. "I do not tolerate—"

Travis stepped aside so Spurl could see me. "We were with Jonah."

"Helping him," Jerry said.

I shrugged. "Sorry we're late, Mr. Spurl."

Spurl frowned. "Well. See that it doesn't happen again."

He pointed to the nearest table. "Sit down so we can get started."

The room was set up with tables and groups of chairs. Travis and Jerry sat down, and I grabbed the seat across from them. Normally I would have sat with Jason and Kevin and Mitch. But I didn't want to press my luck with Spurl.

Tiffany leaned across the aisle. "Jonah Truman. What have you been up to?" I started to say I hadn't been with Travis and Jerry, but Tiffany laughed, and so did Jennifer Knapp, sitting next to her. Usually Tiffany and Jennifer ignored me. I decided to keep my mouth shut.

"Here, Jonah." Jerry dropped a little pile of M&M's in front of me.

"Where'd these come from?"

Jerry laughed. "Some sixth grader dropped them." He held up the bag. "A whole bag of them." Travis laughed, too.

Spurl was handing out worksheets. "I'm giving one to each table. I expect this to be a group effort, with everyone sharing input." He dropped a worksheet on our table. "Do you understand the instructions, Mr. Hunter?"

Travis nodded. "I think so, Mr. Spurl." And, as soon as Spurl was gone, he shot the worksheet over to me. "Here, Mr. Truman. You do it."

It was a worksheet on the Pilgrims. Jill Cunningham tapped my shoulder from the table behind me. I turned around and looked at her and Thuy Ngyuen. "Do it real slow," Jill said. "So Spurl doesn't have as much time to lecture," Thuy added.

I nodded and wrote "Mayflower" in the first blank.

"You ever watch *The Simpsons*, Jonah?" Jerry asked.

I erased "Mayflower" and wrote it again. "Uh, sometimes," I said. I hadn't seen it lately, because Bob liked to watch *Deep Space Nine* instead. I wrote "Plymouth" on the second blank.

Travis nodded. "It was really funny last night. Boobs."

I looked up at him, but before I could say anything, Jerry said, "Boobs," just a little louder.

For a second, I thought they were still talking about the TV show. Or maybe about Tiffany. "What?" I asked.

Travis leaned across the table. "We're playing the boobs game. You have to say it louder than the last person."

"And the first one who gets caught loses." Jerry was grinning. He had chocolate on his front teeth from the candy.

"Boobs?" I said.

Travis laughed. "All right, Jonah. Boobs."

"Boobs," Jerry said.

They both looked at me. I knew if I didn't play, they'd laugh at me. And so would Tiffany and Jen. If I did play and Spurl caught us . . . he'd blame Travis. "Boobs," I said.

"Jonah Truman," Tiffany said again. "You really surprise me." She laughed, and I laughed, too.

It was pretty noisy in the room, and we'd gone around the table at least three times, saying "boobs" louder and louder before Jerry got caught.

"What did you say, Mr. Fitzner?" Spurl asked.

"Oops," Jerry said. "I said oops, because I shared some wrong input."

Behind us, Thuy and Jill giggled, and I knew they knew what was going on, too.

As soon as Spurl started talking to Sylvie's table, we started playing again. Most of the class had caught on, and they were cracking up more than we were. Melanie Bales gave us a dirty look from over in the corner, but I ignored her.

Just as I finished the worksheet, Spurl heard Jerry again.

"I said, I think the answer to number seven is tubes," he told Spurl.

Travis raised his hand. "Like boob tubes, you know?"

Our whole side of the room burst out laughing. It was

11

totally worth Spurl's ten-minute lecture on why the Pilgrims didn't have television sets.

Out in the hall, Jerry said, "You guys were cheating."

"You can't cheat at the boobs game, Fitzner," Travis said.

"It was skill," I said, and Travis laughed and punched me. He punched really hard. I managed to keep from rubbing it.

"Travis!" Tiffany bounced up. "I'll walk you to math." Travis put his arm across her shoulders, and she nestled up against him. They took off, with Jerry trailing after them.

I watched them go, trying to imagine me walking down the hall like that with Katherine Chang. I couldn't do it. I couldn't even imagine it.

The note was in my locker at the end of the day. It was folded into a fat triangle. It took me a while to get it unfolded. Inside it said, "Who would I like to go out with?" And, underneath, it said "Jonah Truman" nineteen times in nineteen different colors of ink. I counted.

It wasn't signed. I turned it over and checked the back, but it was blank. I folded the note carefully and put it in my pocket.

The Solution to All Your Problems

By the time I'd walked home, I'd convinced myself the note probably wasn't from Katherine. Katherine was quiet and serious. She was not the kind of girl who sent notes to boys. It was one of the things I knew I liked about her.

When I got to the end of our driveway, I stopped and pulled the note out and read it one more time. What if it was just somebody's idea of a joke? Kevin and I had put a note something like it in Brandon Ziegler's locker back in sixth grade. And it was exactly the kind of thing Travis and Jerry would think was hilarious.

Mom was in the kitchen when I walked in. "Hi, sweetie. How was your day?" She looked really smiley and happy. It was all I needed right now.

"Eighth grade sucks," I said. I flopped down onto one of the kitchen chairs.

13

She stopped smiling. "You know I hate that word, Jonah." She jabbed at something in the pan on the stove.

"What is that? It smells awful."

She jabbed it again. "It's dinner." She dropped the lid onto the pan and turned to face me. "What's so bad about eighth grade?"

I held up my left hand and counted off on my fingers. "Mrs. Abrams assigned twenty pages of *The Pearl,* due tomorrow. I have thirty-two math problems, due tomorrow. I have to build a weather vane for science." I bent back my little finger especially hard. "And Mr. Spurl . . . Mom, he is *so* boring."

"Jonah," Mom said, "give the man a chance." She teaches fourth grade, and she always thinks teachers deserve a chance.

I knew if you gave Spurl *half* a chance, he'd bore you to death. But I decided not to say it.

"What's that smell?" My little sister, Liz, came into the kitchen.

Mom lifted the lid off the pan, and the smell poured out. Liz held her nose, and even Mom closed her eyes, just for a second.

"What is it?" Liz asked in a nose-pinched voice.

"Bob's mother gave me the recipe." Bob's mother had

flown out for the wedding in July. Ordinarily you don't think about principals even having mothers. Bob's mother had been little and wrinkly and just amazingly old. She'd played Monopoly with Liz and me, and she'd cheated. "It's supposed to be an old family favorite," Mom said. "It's a surprise." She looked in the pan and shook her head. "I know I'm surprised."

"Do we have to eat it?" I asked.

"You have to try it," Mom said. "I'm making plain noodles, too."

"I'm going to eat it," Liz said. "If it's an old family favorite."

I was going to say it wasn't our family, but instead I said, "You'll eat anything Bob eats."

Liz shrugged. "It can't be any worse than tofu tortillas."

I groaned. Liz and I had spent three weeks in Seattle with Dad and his wife, Maureen, and their baby. Maureen was a vegetarian. I'd nearly starved to death. "How about eggplant pasta?" I said.

Liz made a barfing noise.

"I'm sure it wasn't that bad," Mom said, but she was smiling. I knew she sort of liked it when we got going on Maureen.

The doorbell rang.

"I'll get it," Liz shouted, and she dashed out of the room. She was back in a couple of seconds. "It's just Amanda."

"Oh, thanks a lot." Amanda came into the kitchen. She made a face at Liz, and Liz made an uglier face back. They both giggled.

"Hi, Amanda," Mom said. "Jonah was just telling us about eighth grade."

"Oh, it's great," Amanda said. "I love it."

Mom raised her eyebrows at me, but I ignored her.

Amanda was looking around the kitchen. "Something sure smells . . . interesting."

"It's dinner," Mom said.

"Oh. Wow," Amanda said, and Liz and I laughed. Amanda looked at me. "Could I talk to you for a minute?"

We went into the living room. She sat down on the couch, with her legs stuck out. She had a lot of leg to stick out. "This is a great couch," she said. She ran her hand over the cushion next to her. "I've never seen green leather."

"It's Bob's," I said. I sort of missed our old couch. It had sagged in all the right places. The leather couch didn't sag anywhere, and if you weren't careful, you could slide right off onto the floor. I sat down in our old armchair.

16

"Your mom sure seems happier," Amanda said.

I frowned. "Happier than what?"

"You know. Than she was before." Amanda picked up the picture of Mom and Bob and Liz and me off the coffee table. "This is cute. Where was it taken?"

"Multnomah Falls. We've been hiking there three times already." Bob had this thing about bonding in the outdoors.

"Who took the picture?"

"These people Bob stopped." I shook my head, remembering. It had been an old couple, and they'd kept saying what a lovely family we were. It had been totally embarrassing.

Amanda put the picture down. "You know, Melanie's mom got married a couple of years ago to this guy. . . . He's really nice and everything, it's just, he's sort of . . ." She thought for a second. "Chubby? And it's the funniest thing. Because now Melanie and her brother and her mom? They're all . . ."

"Fat?" I said.

"Roly-poly. Just like their stepfather." Amanda grinned at me.

I frowned. "Are you trying to say that Mom and Liz and I are going to look like Bob?"

17

She shrugged. "At least he's not fat."

I had a sudden vision of all of us with frizzy gray hair, wearing sweaters with buttons. I shuddered all over. "Is that what you wanted to talk to me about? Because you didn't have to come all the way over here for that."

"No, no." She leaned forward, and her braid swung over her shoulder. "I have the greatest idea." She grinned. "The solution to all your problems."

I leaned back a little. Sometimes Amanda's ideas did not turn out to be that great. "Not another surefire money-making idea." Amanda and I had had a kind of business going, back before I'd left for Seattle and torture by tofu.

"I'm talking about your love life, dorkus," Amanda said. "What you need is . . ." She opened her arms wide. "Drama club!"

"Drama club?"

"Drama club."

"*Drama* club?"

She punched me, hard, in the leg. "Stop saying that, Jonah. It's really annoying."

"You said it first." I rubbed my leg.

"Look. Ms. Landau is starting an afterschool drama club. Mrs. Manning read about it in the announcements this morning. Weren't you listening?"

18

"Of course I was listening," I said. I just hadn't been paying any attention. "What's the drama club got to do with my love life?"

"Well, a bunch of us were talking about it in French. Emma and Sylvie and Thuy and Katherine and Kevin. We just all thought it sounded like fun."

Why wasn't I taking French? Nobody I knew was taking Spanish. "We're talking about plays and . . . plays. Right?"

"Right."

"And you got Kevin *Martinez* to agree to this?" Kevin and I had been best friends since third grade, and the only thing he'd ever signed up for was time on the computer.

"Well," Amanda said, "he's thinking about it. The thing is, Ms. Landau's going to post a sign-up sheet, and we need to put our names on it right away, before it fills up with sixth graders." She leaned a little closer to me and lowered her voice. "And Katherine said . . ."

The front door opened, and Bob walked in. Amanda sat up straight, and I leaned back in the armchair. Bob stopped in the doorway and smiled at us. "Hi, there."

"Hi, Mr. Decker," Amanda said.

"Hi." Mom came out of the kitchen. She was smiling again. She and Bob hugged and kissed, real quick. No overt displays of affection in the hallway, I thought. But I

19

didn't say it. Amanda was watching them, with a dopey grin on her face.

"Something smells great," Bob said.

"It's your mother's recipe," Mom said. She led him off into the kitchen.

Amanda was still grinning. I punched her on the leg. "So what did Katherine say?"

"Oh." She leaned back closer to me. "Katherine said that she really hoped you'd sign up, too. She said, 'It would be a lot more fun if Jonah was there, too.'"

I felt my face getting very, very hot. "You're sure she said that?"

Amanda groaned and rolled her eyes. "I didn't get it on tape, but I'm sure." She flicked her braid again. "I've told you and told you she likes you. Why don't you just ask her to go out with you? You know you want to."

I sighed. I'd almost asked her, way back last spring. I'd almost asked her during the seventh-grade field trip to the beach. I'd almost asked her on the first day of school. I'd almost asked her today. "I just haven't found the right time yet," I said.

"It's not that hard, Jonah. And it'll be great. I mean, you going out with Katherine, and me going out with Kevin, and we're all friends. We'll be able to do stuff together. It'll be just perfect."

It did sound pretty good. I stood up. "I'll think about this drama thing."

"Katherine really wants to do it." Amanda stood up, too. I realized I was looking right at her nose. Before I'd always been looking at her chin. Maybe I'd grown *three* inches over the summer. "I promise you won't regret it, Jonah. Scout's honor." She held up the fingers of her right hand.

"That's the Vulcan 'Live long and prosper' sign, Amanda."

She looked at her fingers. "No kidding." I was definitely looking right at her nose. She put her fingers over it. "What's wrong? Do I have a zit or something?"

"No. Never mind."

When she was gone, I went upstairs to Mom's room. I sat down on the edge of the bed and tried to visualize myself calling Katherine up and asking her to go out with me. Maureen was big on visualization. "Just see yourself skating, Jonah," she'd said when she'd bought me in-line skates. "Just visualize yourself rolling down the street." I'd rolled right down the street and into a hedge. I folded my arms behind my head and visualized Katherine. And then I realized that I was sitting on Bob's side of the bed. I got up.

There was a big pile of books on the nightstand. The top one had a picture of a woman and a man and a bunch of nerdy kids. The title said, "Blended Families." It reminded me of one of those drinks, where you throw fruit and yogurt and milk all together in the blender. Mom makes them when she's dieting. I hate those drinks.

"Jonah!" Liz shouted. "Dinner's ready!"

Mom had already put food on everybody's plate when I got to the dining room. Brownish-gray lumps in a brownish-gray, gluey sauce. I sat down across from Liz. I made a gagging face, and she laughed.

"How was your day, Ellen?" Bob asked. He took a big bite of lumps.

"Fine," Mom said. "We started planning the potlatch. I had to confiscate two water weenies and a plastic bag full of something called 'Yukko Slimo.'"

"Can I have it?" I asked.

"No. I already threw it away."

Bob looked at Liz. He had this little dinner ritual that he'd probably gotten out of one of the books upstairs. "And how was your day?"

Liz sighed like she was going to say something really sad. "I am the only girl in fourth grade who wears knee socks." She shoved a forkful of lumps around behind her salad.

"Bummer," I said. I took a big bite of plain noodles.

"Stephanie Fraser says only little kids wear knee socks. Stephanie Fraser wears ankle socks with question marks on them." Liz fluffed up her salad.

"Who is Stephanie Fraser?" Mom asked.

"She just moved here from California. She's been to Disneyland fourteen times."

"Wow," I said.

"And she has thirty-two toy cats."

"Wow," Mom and Bob both said.

"So," Liz said, "I need little socks with question marks on them."

Liz and I looked at Mom. She took a bite of salad. Then she sipped at her water. I knew she was going to say, "We'll have to see." But, before she could, Bob said, "Oh, I think we can afford socks with question marks on them."

Liz and I looked at him. He was scraping his fork across his plate.

"She already has several pairs of socks, Bob," Mom said.

"Well, another pair won't hurt." Bob gestured with his fork. "Sometimes these little things can really make a difference, Ellen."

Liz and I looked at Mom. She put a forkful of lumpy stuff in her mouth and chewed for a long time. "We'll have to see," she said finally.

"Well, last but not least." Bob smiled at me. "How was your day, Jonah?"

"Well . . ." I knew Mom was waiting for me to complain about English or the math homework or Spurl. "I think I'm going to join the drama club," I said.

"Drama club?" Mom's fork clanged against her plate.

Bob nodded. "After school. Monday through Thursday." He'd cleaned his plate and was getting seconds. "We got funds for afterschool activities. It's part of the antigang campaign. Stevie Landau has some great ideas."

I didn't have to listen to the announcements. I was living with the announcements.

"Drama club?" Mom said again, and I thought that if Amanda were here, she'd punch her.

"I don't have to do it, Mom."

"No, no. I just didn't know you were interested in drama."

24

I shrugged. "It's kind of a new thing. Amanda and Kevin are doing it."

Bob speared a tomato out of his salad. "Stevie will be glad to have kids like you in there."

I wondered what he meant by that, but I decided I didn't want to ask.

Try It. It's Easy.

Kevin was at his locker when I got to school the next day.

"Drama club," I said.

"Oh, that." He laughed. "It might be okay."

"It might be awful," I said. I pulled open my locker. I was sort of hoping there might be another note, but it was just full of the usual junk.

"Amanda really wants to do it," Kevin said.

"I know." I dug out my science book.

"I dare you," Kevin said.

"I double-dare you."

"I triple-dare you."

We both laughed.

Kevin sighed. "I'll do it if you'll do it," he said.

The only class I had with Katherine was science. If I had drama club with her, too, well, then maybe things would just happen all on their own. "I'm thinking about it," I said.

Kevin pulled a piece of paper out of his notebook. "Look what I got. The cheat codes to *Mortal Doom III*. Eric Ryder gave them to me."

"Eric Ryder?" If Travis was the biggest jerk in the whole school, then Eric Ryder was, hands down, the biggest nerd.

"He's in my English class," Kevin said. "He knows a *lot* about computer games."

"I'll bet he does," I said.

Kevin pointed to the paper. "See. This gives you invisible armor, and this gives you unlimited fire bombs."

Kevin and his computer games drove me a little crazy, mostly because he was way better than me at all of them. "Cool, Kev." The bell rang. "We'd better go."

Before the last period that day, I stopped by the drama room and added my name to the list on the door, right after Katherine's. It seemed like a good sign.

Friday night Bob and Liz went shopping, and on Saturday morning, Liz came downstairs in her new cat sweatshirt and her new little socks with question marks on them. "I want everybody to call me Libby from now on," she said.

Mom glanced at her over the paper. "Why?"

"Because Stephanie told Tara that Liz is a dumb name."

"I should have guessed," Mom said.

Bob had just come in from jogging. He jogged every Saturday morning. He was wearing a Morey Grizzlies T-shirt and a pair of really short shorts. He had big sweat stains under his arms. "You know what I want to do today?" he said. He started rinsing a coffee cup out at the sink. "I want to buy a computer for the house."

Liz and I looked at Mom. She shrugged and nodded.

"All right!" I said. "Let's get some games."

"*Sim Castle,*" Liz said.

"*Fog Quest III,*" I said.

"Wait a minute." Mom folded up the paper. "We're getting this so Bob can do some work at home. It's not going to be a toy."

"Right, Mom," Liz and I both said.

Bob laughed. "I'd better shower," he said. Mom followed him out of the kitchen.

"He has disgustingly hairy legs," Liz said, and she started to giggle.

"Don't be an idiot," I said, but she was right. I was glad he wore long pants to school.

We spent a long time at the computer store. Liz threw a fit because Mom wouldn't let Bob buy the mouse cover that looked like a real mouse. But he did get *Sim Castle* and *Fog Quest III*. I didn't want the stupid mouse cover, anyway.

We lugged about ten boxes into the living room. "I think it will have to go on the desk in here," Bob said. "I don't really want it in our bedroom."

"Definitely not in the bedroom," Mom said.

"Where are the games?" I asked.

"Not in here." Liz was pulling Styrofoam out of a box.

"Hang on there a second. I think we should read the manual first." Bob was holding a book that looked like it weighed about two hundred pounds.

I sat down on the couch. This was going to take forever.

Liz frowned. "When Becky Anderson got a new computer, they just plugged it into the wall, and it worked right away. Nobody had to read the manual."

"Well, this is probably a different kind of computer," Bob said.

"It's a stupid kind of computer."

"Liz," Mom said. "This is a good computer." She

looked at all the boxes. "But I think I'll leave this to you guys. I have things to do in the kitchen." She left.

Liz was ripping the plastic off one of the games.

"Now, don't lose anything in there, Liz," Bob said.

"Libby," Liz said. "Nobody is remembering to call me Libby."

"Oh, by the way." I leaned back and put my hands behind my head. "I want everybody to call me King Jonah from now on."

Bob laughed.

"That's not funny," Liz said.

"I'm sorry, Libby." Bob sat back on his heels. "Look. Why don't you sit down . . . not by Jonah . . . in the chair . . . and watch me unpack the boxes."

"I don't want to watch. I want to help."

"Watching is helping."

"Watching isn't helping," Liz said. "Watching is boring." She stomped out of the room, just missing the box with the disk drive.

Bob sighed. He waved his hand at the boxes and books. "It's just that I want to do this in order. Step by step."

I nodded and watched him open the manual. I always felt sort of weird when I was all alone with Bob. Weekends were the worst, because he was around all the time. I never knew what to talk about. It reminded me of back in elementary school, when sometimes the principal would come and sit at our table at lunch. Amanda had loved it, but I'd hated it. It just ruined a perfectly good lunch period. I stood up. "I think I'll go see if I can help Mom in the kitchen."

Bob didn't look up from the manual.

Mom was stirring something gray and gloppy in a big bowl. She was humming, some old song from the sixties. I remembered what Amanda had said about Mom being happier. I couldn't remember if she'd hummed so much, back before Bob.

I looked in the bowl. "Don't tell me. Another old family favorite."

She laughed. "No. Papier-mâché. We're making masks for the potlatch. I wanted to try it out first at home before I did it with the kids."

In the living room, Bob said, "Aha!" loudly.

Mom slapped a strip of newspaper into the goop. "You're welcome to help."

I sighed. Bob was in the living room. Liz was upstairs whining. The kitchen was arts-and-crafts central. There

31

was no place I could go in the whole house. "I was thinking about going over to the school and skating on the tennis courts," I said.

Mom frowned and looked out the window. She hadn't
been totally thrilled when I'd come home with the skates.

"It's not raining," I said. "I'll wear all the pads. I'll go
slow. I won't talk to strangers. I'll look both ways before I
cross the street."

She laughed. "I was just going to say be home by four."

I left quick, before she could change her mind, and got
my stuff on in the garage. I didn't know if visualizing had
helped, but by the time we'd left Seattle, I was pretty good
on the in-line skates. I'd gotten a lot of practice. There
hadn't been much else to do at Dad's house, except watch
Maureen feed the baby.

Now I skated down our street and out onto Hoodview. I
skated fast, pumping my arms from side to side like the
guys on TV. I kept pace with an old lady in a red pickup
that had to be going at least thirty. She grinned at me and
waved. I waved back as I slowed and made the turn into
Walt Morey's driveway.

The tennis courts were around behind the portables.
The surface on the courts was nice and smooth, and you
could really wheel. I wished Katherine could see me skate.

32

I followed the driveway around the curve toward the back, past the portables. And I stopped.

Travis and Jerry were sitting on the edge of the sidewalk. They were both wearing skates. Jerry was on his knees, rubbing the edge of the curb with a big chunk of wax.

Travis saw me. "Hey, Jonah." Jerry looked up from his waxing. Travis gave me that grin that always makes me a little nervous. He pointed at the curb. "Want to try grinding?"

I'd seen guys doing it, at the playground in Seattle. I'd never tried it. I'd never actually wanted to try it.

Travis skated over and hockey-stopped beside me. "Watch. This is sweet."

He skated a little farther up the driveway, to get up speed. Then he skated, fast, past me, and hopped onto the curb just where the waxing started. The chassis of his skates slid along the wax, smooth and easy. He hopped off at the end and stopped next to Jerry. "Your turn," he said, looking up at me. Jerry grinned.

"Gee," I said. "It looks like a lot of fun, but . . ."

"Try it, Jonah," Jerry said.

"It's easy," Travis said.

I skated back up the driveway, thinking I could keep on going. Thinking that Mom would kill me if I killed myself.

But I stopped, and I turned and skated, fast, back down the driveway. I tried to remember what Travis had done, when he'd jumped exactly and how he'd held his arms.

"Keep your knees bent!" Travis shouted. I hopped up onto the edge of the curb.

And it worked. I felt my skates hit the wax, and they slid smooth and fast along the surface. I put my arms out to balance and, for a few seconds, it was just like flying.

And then, suddenly, I *was* flying, flying through the air, and I landed, hard, on my hands and knees on the sidewalk.

"Whoa," Jerry said in a quiet voice.

For a second, nothing hurt. I just lay there, thinking well, I'm not dead, and nothing's broken. Thank you, Maureen, for buying the expensive knee pads. And then the palms of my hands started to throb, and then they burned, and then they ached. And then my whole body sort of throbbed and burned and ached. I rolled over on my back, pulled my knees up to my chest and clutched my hands between them.

"Whoa," Jerry said again. He and Travis skated over to me. "Are you okay?" Jerry asked.

"Yeah," I said. I looked at my palms. They were both scraped and bleeding. I rolled over and stood up. "I'm

34

fine." I jammed my hands into the pockets of my jacket.

Travis punched me on the shoulder, and that hurt, too. "You did great, Jonah. You just shoulda kept your knees bent."

I nodded. "Right. I'll remember that." I looked at Jerry. "Your turn."

Jerry laughed. "No way. I'm not crazy." He flicked up the sleeve of his sweatshirt and checked his watch. "It's been twenty minutes."

"Let's go then," Travis said. He skated around the portable toward the front of the school.

Jerry grinned at me. "This is great," he said. "Come on."

I followed him.

We went past the front of the school and around to the side parking lot. The custodian's van was there. A black Volkswagen Jetta was parked next to it.

"Nice car," I said.

"It's Spurl's," Travis said. He shook his head. "Can you believe Spurl drives a car like that? Watch this." He bumped off the sidewalk and skated across the parking lot to the Jetta. He skated around it in a big circle, and, as he came past the driver's door, he slapped it hard with his hand.

The car alarm went off, a loud, blaring honking that I bet you could hear all the way back to my house.

Jerry grabbed my arm and pulled me back behind the corner of the building. Travis skated over to us, fast. He was laughing so hard he nearly slipped and fell.

The door at the side of the school opened, and Spurl came running out. We all pulled back, quick, so he couldn't see us. Jerry peeked around the corner. "He's standing there looking around," he whispered. He laughed softly. "He looks *so* ticked. Now he's walking over to the car. He's looking under it." Jerry started to laugh so hard he couldn't talk.

I peeked over his shoulder. Spurl was lying on the ground looking under the car like he thought somebody was hiding there. Then he stood up and stared around the parking lot, his hands on his hips. Finally he unlocked the door and turned off the alarm. He stomped back into the building.

Travis was shaking his head and laughing. "What a fool," he said.

"How many times have you done it?" I asked.

"Three," Travis said. "Any normal person would stop setting the stupid alarm."

"What's he doing here on a Saturday, anyway?" Jerry asked.

"His wife probably threw him out," I said. "He was probably boring her to death."

Travis and Jerry both laughed. I grinned.

"Come on," Jerry said. "Let's go back by the portables."

My hands were really aching. "You know," I said, "I think I've gotta head home."

Travis looked at me. "Maybe next time we can bring our sticks. Play some hockey."

I didn't have a stick, and I'd never played hockey. But it sounded a lot safer than grinding. "Sure," I said. "Next time."

When I got home, Mom and Bob were moving the desk to the other side of the living room. It kind of stuck out funny, and it was going to make it way harder to get at the CD player, but before I could say anything, Bob said, "Were you over at the school, Jonah?"

"Yeah," I said. "For a little while."

"I just got a phone call from Ron Spurl. Seems he's been over there, and someone's been messing with his car. I thought maybe you might have seen something."

I put my head on one side, like I was thinking about this

very hard. "I was over by the tennis courts," I said, finally. "On the far side of the portables." I held up my hands. "I fell."

"Oh, Jonah!" Mom put down her end of the desk and came over to look. She shook her head. "We'll have to put something on those scrapes."

I looked at Bob over her shoulder. "By the way," I said, "I really need a hockey stick."

Will There Be Kissing?

Sunday afternoon, Bob and I went to the sporting-goods store, and he bought me a stick and some street hockey balls. He didn't mention anything about the school or Spurl's car.

Amanda called me that night. Liz had to come get me out on the driveway where I was practicing slap shots.

"Don't forget," Amanda said, "drama club starts tomorrow after school."

"I know, Amanda."

"And you aren't going to chicken out?"

"No, I'm not going to chicken out."

"Good," she said, "because I told Katherine you're going to be there. You don't want to disappoint her." She laughed as she hung up.

The sign on the drama-room door said, "Leave it at the door." I didn't know what it meant, but I went inside anyway.

The drama room was huge, and all the tables and chairs were pushed to one side, to make a big space in the middle. Ms. Landau was sitting cross-legged on top of a table near the door. She was wearing blue jeans and a red T-shirt that said VAN HALEN in white letters. It was a really tight T-shirt. "Welcome," she said, and she gave me a big smile. She had a lot of straight, white teeth.

I looked around the room. Kids were sitting in bunches on the floor. Most of them were eighth-graders. Most of them were girls. Emma and Sylvie and Thuy were squished together in a corner. They waved, and I waved back.

Katherine and Amanda and Kevin were sitting on the floor next to the filing cabinet. "Over here," Amanda said, and she wiggled closer to Kevin so I sort of had to sit down next to Katherine.

Amanda leaned across Katherine and punched my knee. "This is going to be so cool," she said. She looked at Katherine. "Isn't this cool?"

Katherine nodded. "It is. I'm really glad you talked me into it."

Talked her into it? Amanda had told me Katherine really wanted to do it. I glared at Amanda, but she was looking at Kevin.

Katherine smiled at me. I stopped glaring and smiled back. All of a sudden, my stomach growled, a long, low rumble.

"What?" Katherine leaned toward me a little.

"What?" I said. I put my hand over my stomach.

"Did you say something?"

"Uh . . . no. I didn't say anything."

"Oh. I thought you did."

I shook my head. She smelled like the cookies Grandma makes at Christmas. I knew I was blushing a bright red. I wondered if maybe one of the things we'd learn in drama club was how not to blush. I wondered if I'd remembered to put deodorant on after P.E.

Eric Ryder walked in with a bunch of seventh-graders. He was wearing a pair of blue plaid shorts and a striped shirt. He had a Star Trek communicator pinned to the shirt. Amanda and I both looked at Kevin.

Kevin shrugged. "He asked me what I was doing after school."

"Hey, Kevin." Eric shoved himself down in between Kevin and the filing cabinet. "I've been thinking, and I *know* the Death Star would totally annihilate the *Enterprise.*"

Kevin shook his head. "You haven't read the specs for the *Enterprise.* Its shields are impenetrable."

Amanda put her hand on Kevin's shoulder. "Guys. I have really bad news." Kevin and Eric both looked at her. "The Death Star and the *Enterprise?*" Amanda lowered her voice. "They aren't real!" she shouted suddenly.

Kevin and Eric laughed like she'd said something really funny, and then they turned back and started arguing again.

Amanda looked at Katherine and me and rolled her eyes.

"Eric's been following Kevin around for a week," Katherine whispered. Her breath tickled my ear. "It's driving Amanda absolutely crazy."

I nodded. Amanda looked pretty crazy. "My locker is next to Kevin's," I whispered back.

"Oh, poor Jonah." Katherine looked really concerned and sympathetic, and just for a second, she rested her hand on my knee. I tried to think of something else to say to make her feel sorry for me.

The door opened, and Travis walked in.

The room had been kind of noisy, with everybody talking and messing around. But now it got very quiet. You could hear Sylvie say, "Oh great," really clearly.

Travis grinned. "I am great, aren't I?"

"Travis Hunter. As I live and breathe." Ms. Landau was smiling, and I had to give her a couple of points. It's not every teacher who would look that happy about having Travis in her classroom.

"His name wasn't on the sign-up sheet," Melanie Bales said.

Travis looked at Ms. Landau. "Jeff said I should check this out." Jeff Parker was the art teacher. He let the kids in Art III call him by his first name, and he drove a 1957 red T-bird in mint condition.

"I'll have to thank Mr. Parker for the recommendation," Ms. Landau said. "Now take a seat. We're about to get started."

Travis looked around the room. He was wearing baggy denim shorts, low on his hips, and a T-shirt with a Smelly Tuna snowboard logo. He'd shaved the lower part of his hair over the weekend, and the upper stuff flopped down perfectly. Never in a million years would I get mine to do that. Tiffany was sitting across the room, and she made room for him next to her. But Travis sat down beside me. Amanda and Katherine both groaned.

Travis leaned back on his hands and stretched his legs out into the room. He had lots of hair on his legs. Not as much as Bob, but lots more than most guys.

"How's it going?" he said.

"Okay. Not bad." My legs looked pale and bald and stubby next to his. I reminded myself to never wear shorts again, no matter how hot it was.

He leaned out a little and looked at Kevin and Eric. "I was afraid this was going to be the total land of nerds."

Eric was showing Kevin something in a *Star Wars* book. "See. Ranges of radioactivity." Only when Eric said it, it sounded more like "wanges of wadioactivity."

Travis leaned out farther. "How's it going, Eh-wick? Eh-wick Wyder?"

Eric and Kevin both ignored him.

Travis poked me in the ribs. "Guess what Eric's favorite dog is?"

"Eric's favorite dog?" I had no idea where Travis was going with this.

"A rottweiler," he said. He looked at Eric. "Isn't that wight, Wyder?"

Eric frowned. "A wottwei—" he started. Then he stopped, and his face flushed an ugly, dark red.

"Jonah," Amanda said. She gave me a really dirty look.

"I didn't do anything," I said, but Katherine put her finger to her lips and pointed at Ms. Landau.

"All right. I think everybody's here." Ms. Landau clapped her hands and hopped off the table. She started talking about how glad she was to see us and what she hoped we'd get out of the club. She paced back and forth as she talked and moved her hands around a lot.

"Van Halen?" Katherine whispered.

Amanda shrugged. "How old do you think she is?"

"Twenty-five, maybe?" Katherine whispered back. She glanced at me like she thought I'd know. I shrugged.

"Sylvie said she's not married," Amanda said.

"Do you think she's dating?" Katherine asked.

Before Amanda could answer, Travis tapped me on the shoulder. "Do you think she's wearing a bra?" he whispered.

Amanda and Katherine both looked like Travis had said . . . well . . . exactly what he'd said. I laughed. I couldn't help it.

"Is there something you want to share with the rest of us, Jonah?" Ms. Landau asked. She didn't say it like Spurl would. She really sounded sort of hopeful.

I shook my head. "I don't think so," I said slowly. Travis snickered, and Amanda and Katherine both scooted away from me.

"Well, then." Ms. Landau clapped her hands again. "Enough sitting around. Drama is physical." She spread the word out like it had fifteen syllables.

We all stood up, and she led us through some stretches and warm-ups like Mr. Adams does when we're going to run the mile. But she even had us warm up our faces, sticking out our tongues and wiggling our eyebrows and bugging out our eyes. Only everybody started laughing, and we had to quit.

She made us stand in a circle, and we had to take turns saying our names three times in different ways, shouting or whispering or singing. I'd never realized how dumb "Jonah" sounded until I had to say it out loud three times.

Then we played a game where we pretended to throw an invisible ball around the room. Ms. Landau kept saying, "Good energy!" And when we were done, she clapped her hands and said, "Good risk-taking, group!"

I ended up standing right next to Katherine. "I feel *so* dumb," she said.

"I feel like a total idiot," I said.

"You are a total idiot, Jonah." Travis put his arm around

46

my shoulders and pulled me closer so he could punch me in the ribs. By the time I'd managed to pull free, Katherine was back over by Amanda.

Travis draped his arm across Tiffany's shoulders. He didn't punch her in the ribs, and Tiffany didn't try to pull loose. "I thought drama was plays and stuff," Travis said.

Somebody laughed, a nasty kind of laugh. Ms. Landau put out a hand. "You're absolutely right, Travis."

"So what do these games have to do with drama?"

Somebody—and I was beginning to suspect it was Amanda—laughed again, like this was a totally dumb question. Ms. Landau clapped her hands, and said, "Good question. Let's sit down and discuss it."

Everybody sort of flopped down where they were, except I noticed the girls clumped up together on the other side of the room. Only Tiffany sat down with the boys, next to Travis.

I stared at Katherine, sitting across the room next to Amanda, and tried to send psychic waves to get her to look at me and smile. But she kept looking at Ms. Landau. Emma smiled at me, though, and crossed her eyes, and I smiled back.

Travis and Tiffany started playing thumb war. Travis won three games, and then he let Tiffany win one.

47

"Will there be kissing?" one of the seventh-grade girls asked, and all the other girls laughed.

I stopped watching Travis and Tiffany and looked at Ms. Landau.

"Well," she said, "let's not worry about that right now."

"What are they talking about?" I whispered to Kevin.

"I have no idea," he said, and I realized he'd been watching Travis and Tiffany, too.

"*Romeo and Juliet,* you dopes," Eric said.

I felt a strange sort of hot and cold feeling, like maybe I'd just come down with the flu. *Romeo and Juliet*? Katherine was smiling, but Amanda had a funny look on her face, like she'd just eaten a bug.

"I'm really excited about this project, guys," Ms. Landau was saying. "It fits in perfectly with the state-mandated gangs curriculum. I've found a really good shortened version of the play. And . . ." She smiled like she was going to tell us the permanent cure for zits or something else really wonderful. "And one of the theaters downtown is going to let me borrow some of their old costumes."

The girls all murmured, like she *had* told us the cure for zits. Even Amanda smiled.

"But first," Ms. Landau said, "we'll be spending time on theater games and exercises and just generally getting to know each other much better." She looked around at all of us. "Are there any questions?" There weren't. Ms. Landau sighed and clapped her hands. "Well, then. I guess we're done for the day."

Everybody got up. The girls crowded together into little clumps, talking about parts and costumes.

"*Romeo and Juliet*'s not really that bad," Eric said. "There's swordfighting, and lots of people die. I saw the movie on TV."

"Swordfighting," Travis said. "That would be sweet."

"In the new movie, they shoot each other," Tiffany said. She wrapped her arms around Travis's arm. "Wouldn't it be great if I got to be Juliet and you were Romeo?"

"Travis will have to be one of the adults," Emma said. She'd come up with Sylvie. "Because he's so tall."

Travis grinned. "That means Katherine will have to be one of the little kids." For a second, I was afraid he was going to say something about me, too, but he didn't.

"There aren't any little kids in *Romeo and Juliet*," Eric said, but everybody ignored him.

"Well, *somebody* has to be Romeo," Tiffany said, "and

it's not like there's a lot of guys to choose from."

"Thanks a lot," Kevin said. Amanda patted him on the arm.

"I'd rather be Tybalt or Mercutio," Eric said. "They both get to die, and they don't have to kiss anybody." He made a gagging noise. It reminded me of something Liz would do.

"Jonah could be Romeo," Emma said, and she grinned.

"No way," I said.

"Don't want to kiss anybody, Jonah?" Travis asked, and he made the same noise Eric had made.

"It's not that," I said. "But I'm not going to be Romeo."

"If you're catching the activities bus," Ms. Landau said, "you'd better get moving."

Everybody started grabbing their stuff and heading for the door. Travis went out with his arm around Tiffany. I wondered how they could walk without tripping over each other's feet.

Amanda followed me out into the hall. "*Romeo and Juliet,*" she said.

I laughed. "You should have seen the look on your face."

She made the same face again. "It's not exactly what I was expecting."

"What were you expecting?"

"Not that. I should have joined the Volleyball Club instead."

I looked up at her. "You're not going to quit, are you?"

"Of course not." She looked at me. "Are you?"

I thought about it. "No. Actually, I sort of had an okay time."

She waggled her eyebrows. "Like talking to Katherine?"

"Yeah," I said. "Yeah. That was okay, too."

Amanda laughed. "Jonah Truman. There's hope for you yet."

Still Friends

There was a note in my locker first thing on Tuesday. It was folded into a long, skinny fan. Inside it said, "Jonah. I am in French. Mrs. Hassel spits when she talks. It's totally disgusting. I am so glad you're doing drama. I think you'll make a great Romeo." It wasn't signed, but underneath there was a picture of Mrs. Hassel spitting. It was pretty funny.

Kevin looked around his open locker door. "What is that?"

I held it out to him. "A note."

He read it and laughed. "That's good. Hassel does spit all the time. Nobody wants to sit in the front row." He turned the note over. "Who wrote it?"

"I don't know." I took it back. "Is there somebody in your French class who draws pictures like this?"

"I don't know, Jonah. It's a big class. And Mrs. Hassel teaches more than one, you know." Kevin slammed his locker shut. "It could be from Mitch Norton. He draws pictures all the time."

"Mitch Norton draws pictures of cars, Kevin. And, anyway, he's not in drama."

Kevin shrugged. "Still. It could be a lot of people."

"But not a guy," I said. "Some *guy* isn't going to be glad I'm Romeo."

"I don't know, Jonah. You're pretty cute," Kevin said.

"Moron." I hit him in the chest, and I saw he was wearing a Star Trek pin. "Where did you get that?"

"At the mall. On Saturday. Eric and I were looking at video games at Egghead."

"You and Eric were at the mall?"

"Yeah. He spent the night Friday night."

I used to spend the night at Kevin's. I flicked the pin with my finger. "It's pretty nerdy, Kev."

He shrugged. "I like it."

In drama that day, we played a bunch of Ms. Landau's screwy games, and on Wednesday we did what she called improv skits. We didn't have lines or anything. She told us what we were supposed to be, and then we made stuff up. I got to be a policeman pulling Kevin and Emma and

Tiffany over for speeding. And then I was in an ice-cream store with Amanda and Eric and two of the seventh-graders. It was more fun than I expected, even though Eric got really stupid and pretended to be a Klingon. He kept shouting, "There is no honor in Rocky Road." Only Ms. Landau laughed.

Amanda caught up with me out on the sidewalk when we were all done. "Katherine says I should tell you that you did a great job today. The cop thing. That was great."

I shrugged. "It was all right." Although I had thought it was pretty good.

"And?" Amanda raised her eyebrows.

"And what?"

"And now what are you going to say that I can tell Katherine?"

"Oh. Oh. Tell her thanks a lot."

"Jonah!" Amanda punched me, hard, in the shoulder.

"Ow! Why'd you do that?"

"Because you don't say thanks. You say something nice about her. Like I told you she said she liked your hair and your T-shirt. Now you say something about her. I'm getting really tired of making things up, Jonah."

I sighed. "What things are you making up?"

Amanda sighed and shoved at her hair. "Not big things.

54

I told her you like her hair, and I told her you thought she looked really good last Wednesday."

"Why last Wednesday?"

"She had on that black skirt and the sleeveless sweater?"

"Oh, oh yeah." She had looked great. And I did like her hair. Katherine had incredible hair. "Those are okay," I said. I patted her on the shoulder. "Keep up the good work, Amanda."

She punched me again, even harder. I wondered if she'd been working out or something. "You have to help me out here, Jonah."

"Okay. Okay." I thought for a minute. "Tell her . . . tell her . . ."

"That you liked the thing she did with Travis? Where she was the mom?" Amanda had her hands on her hips.

"Yeah. Yeah. Tell her that was good." I snapped my fingers. "Tell her she had great energy."

Amanda sighed. "I'll tell her you thought she was cute."

I nodded. "That would be okay, too."

I knew Amanda must have talked to her, because Katherine gave me a big smile when she walked into drama the next day. Only Sylvie was telling Thuy and Emma and me why she hated Evan Gillespie, and all I could do was smile back.

Ms. Landau clapped her hands. "Today we're going to do some experiments in moving." She was wearing a gauzy sort of skirt that you could almost see through.

"I hope she moves in front of the windows," Travis said over my shoulder.

I laughed. "Jonah!" Emma gave me a little shove, but she was laughing, too.

First we had to move around the room like different kinds of animals. And then we had to move like fruits and vegetables. "If fruits and vegetables could move," Ms. Landau said quickly, when Eric's hand went up.

Finally we did people. "How does a homeless person walk? How would you walk if you'd just won the gold medal in the Olympics? How do people you know at home or at school move?" Ms. Landau said.

It was actually kind of fun, although, with everybody moving around at once, the hardest part was to keep from running into people.

After a while, Ms. Landau clapped her hands and said, "Good energy. Good risk-taking. Now, let's all sit down and see if anybody would like to share their experiments with the group."

Amanda and Katherine sat down next to me. "This sort of reminds me of kindergarten," Amanda said.

"Just like show-and-tell," Katherine said.

It didn't remind me of show-and-tell. I'd liked show-and-tell. Standing up there all alone in front of a bunch of middle-school kids seemed a lot different from kindergarten.

Melanie was waving her hand back and forth. "Ah," Ms. Landau smiled. "A volunteer."

Melanie started sliding across the floor. "Don't tell us what you are," Ms. Landau said. "Let us guess."

And everybody said, "A snake," at the same time. Melanie looked really ticked that we'd guessed so fast.

One of the seventh-graders did her little brother, which was actually kind of funny. Sylvie did a cherry tomato. Then Travis did a football player after winning a game.

When Travis was done, Emma started waving her hand back and forth. But, when Ms. Landau called on her, Emma said, "I don't want to do mine. But Jonah was doing something really cool. Back before we quit?"

Everybody looked at me. "Would you like to share, Jonah?" Ms. Landau asked.

Travis gave me a shove. "Go on, Jonah. Before the cherry tomato comes back."

The center of the room seemed a lot bigger when you were standing up there all alone. Katherine was smiling at

57

me, and so was Emma. I gave her a dirty look, and she frowned.

My face felt really hot, and my hands were cold. I tried to remember exactly what I'd been doing. I started walking kind of fast and bent forward, with my feet turned really far out. Halfway across the circle, I remembered to put my hands on my hips. And, when I straightened up and turned, my head cocked to one side, and pointed my finger, everybody said, "Mr. Decker!" And Amanda said, "Mr. Decker yelling at Travis." And they all laughed, even Ms. Landau. Some of them even clapped.

"Do it tonight, Jonah, at dinner," Sylvie said.

"Yeah. Well. I'll think about," I said, and they all laughed again.

I didn't do my Bob impression at dinner. When Mom asked him how *his* day had been, he just rubbed the bridge of his nose and sighed. "The usual," he said.

The phone rang after dinner. I grabbed it in Mom's bedroom.

"Hey. It's me," Travis said.

"Hey."

"I was wondering if you could play hockey on Saturday."

"Oh. Yeah. I think so."

"Okay," Travis said. "Two o'clock." And he hung up.

I was thinking maybe I'd go out and practice my shots when the phone rang again.

"Hi!"

It was definitely a girl. Not Amanda and not Katherine. "Hi," I said slowly.

"This is Sylvie."

"Oh. Hi." I sat down on the floor by the bed. "What's up?"

"Well," Sylvie said, "I'm actually not the one who's calling you."

"You're not?"

"No. Emma's really calling you."

"She is?" Someone giggled. Not me and not Sylvie. "Is Emma at your house?"

"No. See. I have conference calling. I'm at my house, and Emma's at her house, and you're at your house."

I leaned over and pushed the bedroom door shut. "So. Why's Emma calling me?"

Emma giggled again, and nobody said anything. All I could hear was a lot of breathing.

"Emma's afraid you're mad at her," Sylvie said finally.

"I'm not afraid he's *mad* at me," Emma said.

"That's what you told me," Sylvie said.

59

"I did not," Emma said.

I wiggled my foot over against the door, so I could hold it shut. "Why would I be mad in the first place?"

"Because of that thing in drama club," Sylvie said. "Telling Ms. Landau that you should do your walking thing."

"Movement experiment," I said, stretching the syllables out like Ms. Landau, and they both laughed.

"Emma's afraid you totally hate her, and that you'll never speak to her again," Sylvie said.

I laughed. "I don't totally hate you, Emma."

"Well," Sylvie said, "if she hadn't gone and opened her big mouth . . ."

"I don't have a big mouth," Emma said. "I just really thought that Jonah was so good. I mean, way better than Melanie."

"Oh, please," Sylvie said.

"I'm really not mad, Emma," I said. "And I don't hate you. It was fun. I was glad you said something."

"Oh, good." Emma heaved a big sigh. "So we're still friends and everything?"

I wasn't sure what "and everything" meant. And all of a sudden, I wanted to ask her if she had nineteen colored pens. But not with Sylvie listening. Because maybe it wasn't Emma. Maybe Emma hadn't sent me the notes.

"Are we still friends?" Emma asked again.

"Sure," I said. "Sure. We're friends."

"Oh, good," Emma said, and Sylvie laughed.

Something pushed against the door. "Hey!" Liz shouted. "The door's stuck."

"I'm on the phone!" I shouted. Emma and Sylvie both giggled.

"I have to call Stephanie!"

"I'm using the phone!"

"Mom!" Liz shrieked. "Jonah's locked in your bedroom, and he won't let me in!"

Emma and Sylvie giggled again.

"I gotta go," I said.

"Okay. See you tomorrow," Emma said.

"Right. See you tomorrow."

"Bye," Sylvie said.

As soon as I hung up, I realized that they were probably still connected, probably talking about me. I picked up the phone quick, but all I heard was the dial tone.

Liz punched me when I let her in. I made a grab for her, but she was too quick. She stuck out her tongue and slammed the door. I went downstairs.

Bob was sitting cross-legged in the middle of the floor.

Pieces of the computer were strewn all around him. "The manual says this is the right plug," he muttered.

Mom was sitting on the couch with a bowl of popcorn. "Want some?"

I shook my head. Bob liked cheese on his popcorn. It smelled like dirty sweat socks.

"Who was on the phone?" Mom asked.

I thought about it. "Travis," I said.

"Travis *Hunter?*" Mom asked, as if I knew fifteen guys named Travis.

Bob glanced up. "I didn't know you knew Travis."

Mom sighed. "Oh, I know Travis. I had him in fourth grade. It was the year I seriously thought about quitting teaching and taking a job at the bank."

Bob laughed. "He's not really a bad kid. I mean, compared to some. He's just a challenge."

"He can disrupt a class faster than any kid I ever saw. And he's a bully. I'll never forget when he made Brent Murray eat dirt at recess, and then Brent threw up during music."

"That sounds like Travis," Bob said.

I cleared my throat, loudly. "He wants me to play hockey with him on Saturday. Over at the school. And I won't eat any dirt."

Bob laughed, but Mom didn't. "You and Travis?" she said.

"And Jerry Fitzner."

"And Jerry Fitzner," Mom said, and she sighed.

"Don't forget we're having dinner with Doug and Diane on Saturday." Bob smiled at me. "Cooper and Tucker are really looking forward to seeing you."

I couldn't figure out how Bob could have ended up with such obnoxious grandkids. "I'm looking forward to seeing them," I said. I looked at Mom. "I'll be back way before dinner."

Mom was still frowning. "Well, I suppose it will be all right."

"Okay," I said. As I left the room, I heard Bob say, "I really don't think you have to worry about Travis, Ellen."

And Mom said, "It's not Travis I'm worried about."

Jell-O Salad

I'd spent every afternoon that week practicing my hockey shots. Bob never said that the ball hitting the garage door drove him crazy, but on Friday evening he bought me a net.

I left the house early on Saturday. I wanted to warm up on the tennis courts before Travis and Jerry got there. By the time they skated through the gate, I was feeling pretty good. "Let's play some hockey," I said.

"I'll be the goalie," Jerry said. He didn't have the pads, but he did have gloves and a helmet with a faceguard.

Travis had brought two water bottles, and we used those to mark a goal. Jerry skated over in between them, and Travis and I played one-on-one.

I was glad I'd practiced. Travis was good, and he had a

great slap shot. I could outmaneuver him, though. Being small had *some* advantages.

We took a break when the score was tied at 6 to 6, and Travis started showing me how to do wrist shots. After about fifteen minutes, I managed to get my stick right behind the ball. The ball shot past Jerry's right shoulder. It hit the fence with a bang and stuck fast in one of the holes in the chain link.

Travis slapped me on the back so hard he nearly knocked me over. "Truman has a gun!" he said.

"A gun and a half," Jerry said.

I grinned. I felt really good. Even better than when I'd finally managed to beat Kevin at *Air Hawks*. "How do you know all this stuff?" I asked Travis.

Travis skated around behind Jerry and pried the ball out of the fence. "My dad taught me. He used to play junior ice hockey when he was a kid. He was going to be a pro and everything." Travis dropped the ball and shot it, hard, all the way across the court. "He's a lawyer in Spokane instead."

Jerry laughed. "Jeez. I'd rather be a hockey player any day."

Travis shrugged. "Yeah. Well. My dad's a jerk." He skated after the ball. "Let's play some more."

At 3:30, Jerry said he had to quit. "I have to go to church."

I'd just made a great shot, and the ball bounced against the fence. I skated around Jerry to snag it. "Are you sure? Can't you stay a little longer?"

"Naw. I really gotta go."

Travis skated over and picked up the water bottles. He took a big swig out of one, then handed the other one to me. "You've got good ball-handling skills, Jonah."

Jerry snickered. "Ball handling," he said. He looked at me, and I started to laugh. The water splooshed out of my mouth and down my shirt, which made Jerry laugh even harder.

"Ball handling isn't funny, Fitzner," Travis said.

Jerry and I both started laughing hysterically. Jerry's skates started to slip, and he grabbed me, and I grabbed him, and we both fell down in a pile.

Travis shook his head. "What a pair of idiots." He gave me a hand and pulled me up. "You want to come over to my house for a Coke or something?"

"Sure," I said.

Travis lived in one of the big houses in the new development that had gone in on 127th.

"Hey," I said as we skated down the sidewalk. "I re-

66

member when this was a big field. My mom and I used to pick blackberries here."

Travis glanced back over his shoulder. "No blackberries now," he said. "Everybody sprayed them with plant death."

"Yeah. Well." I felt sort of sad. "They were good blackberries."

We took our skates off on the Hunters' front porch. Travis's mother was sitting in the living room, watching TV. I recognized her from school. I'd seen her coming out of Bob's office. She hit the "pause" on the remote, and the picture froze on some woman hugging a man and crying. Travis's mother gave us a big smile. "Who's your friend, Travis?"

I didn't realize she meant me until Travis said, "Jonah."

"I'm glad to meet you, Jonah." For a second, I thought she was going to get up and shake my hand. I noticed my socks were kind of sweaty, and I was leaving damp footprints on the clean hardwood floor.

But she didn't get up. "Where do you live?"

"Over by the school. Off Hoodview."

"Jonah's in drama club," Travis said. He grabbed my arm. "Come on. Coke's in the kitchen."

The kitchen was white, except for a bowl of green apples

sitting on the counter. A big family room stretched off from one end, and it was mostly white, too. A huge TV stood in one corner. "Wow," I said.

"My stepdad got it for football," Travis said. He dug around in the fridge and handed me a Coke. "He moved out, though. Last month. He's probably going to take the TV back."

"Oh. Too bad." I didn't know what else to say.

Travis shrugged. "No big loss." He walked over and clicked the TV on with a remote on the coffee table. "I will miss the TV, though," he said.

He sat down on the couch. I sat down next to him. I took a little sip of the Coke. I sort of had to go to the bathroom.

Travis was flicking through the channels. He stopped at an old show. "All right. *The A-Team.*" He put his feet up on the coffee table. "What do you think of drama club?"

"It's okay. I guess," I added, in case he hated it.

He nodded, though. "Good way to meet girls." He nudged me with his elbow, and some of the Coke sloshed onto my hand. "I've been hearing stuff about you and Katherine Chang. She's pretty cute."

"Yeah. She is." I licked at the Coke. I wanted to ask him

what things he'd heard, but I was afraid he'd ask me if they were true.

"She's kind of quiet," Travis said.

"Kind of."

Travis drained his Coke. "But she sure has great hair." He burped, really long and loud. "Whoa. I feel better."

I laughed. He stood up and threw the can toward the kitchen sink. The back door opened, and Travis's brother, Cody, walked in. The can missed the sink. It hit Cody right in the side of the head.

"Hey!" Cody shouted. He was at least a foot taller than Travis and way heavier. People at Walt Morey still talked about Cody Hunter. He picked up the can and threw it back at Travis, as hard as he could. Travis ducked, and the can bounced off the TV and landed in the fireplace.

"What is going on?" Their mother was standing in the doorway. She pointed at Cody. "This is exactly the kind of thing that drove Brian crazy."

Travis groaned, but Cody laughed. "Mom. Brian was crazy way before he moved in here."

"I don't want to hear it, Cody." She looked at me like she'd forgotten who I was. Then she smiled. "Would you like to stay for dinner, Jonah?"

I put my Coke down on the coffee table and stood up. "I really have to get home," I said.

Travis followed me to the front door. "Don't mind my mother," he said. "She's nuts."

I pulled my skates on. "No problem," I said. "See you Monday."

Mom was in the kitchen when I got home. She was stringing noodles on a piece of yarn. She looked up at me. "How was hockey?"

"Okay. Where is everybody?"

"Liz is upstairs and Bob . . ." She frowned, and just for a second, I remembered the way she used to look at Dad sometimes. "Bob is at the store buying salad. Bob forgot to tell me that he told Diane we'd bring the salad."

I scratched under my shirt. "I think maybe I'll go take a shower."

She jabbed another noodle onto the yarn. "I hate potlatches," she muttered.

Bob was back by the time I'd showered and changed. He was in the kitchen with Mom and Liz. They were staring at a container from the deli.

"Jell-O salad?" Mom said.

"Well, all the green salads looked kind of limp, and I

didn't think the kids would eat cucumbers in yogurt." Bob looked at Liz and me.

He was right about that. Of course, I wasn't going to eat red Jell-O with big chunks of something white and gooey in it, either.

"I'm allergic to Jell-O," Liz said.

"Nobody's allergic to Jell-O," I said. She kicked me, hard. I made a grab for her, but she ducked around the table.

"Guys," Mom said.

Bob held up the container. "We'll just put this into one of our bowls, and we'll tell Diane it's an old family recipe."

"Bob Decker," Mom said. Her voice was low and tight, and I stopped with my hands on Liz's shoulders. I hadn't heard her sound really mad in a long time. "Don't you dare try to pass that off as something I made." She shoved the container back at him.

"Ellen," Bob said. "Diane loves you. She isn't judging you by your salad." He tried to put his arm around her, but she took a step back. She picked up her purse from the table. "I don't want to be late," she said.

Mom drove. Bob sat in the seat beside her. They were both very quiet.

Liz leaned over from her side of the backseat. "They're having a fight," she whispered.

Her breath was hot and wet. "Don't spit in my ear." I gave her a shove.

She shoved me back. "I'm not spitting!"

"You just did it again!" I wiped spit off my cheek and tried to wipe it on her. She shrieked and slapped at my hand.

I saw Mom start to turn toward us, but before she could say anything, Bob whipped around. "Liz! Cut it out! Right now!" He had a loud voice, and in the closed car it was really loud.

Liz and I both froze. Then she slumped back into her corner.

Bob turned back around. I grinned at Liz and stuck my tongue out at her, but she turned her face to the window.

Mom and Bob were both smiling when Diane opened the door of her house. "Jell-O salad," Bob said, and he handed over the container.

"Really?" Diane looked at the little white box like it might be ticking or something.

Mom patted her arm. "Your father will explain all about it." She looked at Bob and laughed, and he laughed. It made me sort of mad. They hadn't spoken to each other all the way from our house because of this stupid salad, and now it was all like this great joke they'd been working on for hours.

"Grandpa!" Tucker and Cooper came pounding down the stairs and sort of launched themselves onto Bob. He laughed and hugged them.

"And don't forget Grandma," Diane said. I laughed, I couldn't help it, and Mom gave me a dirty look. Diane put her hand on Mom's arm and pulled her toward the kids. Mom had the little lines by her mouth that she gets around Diane. "See. Here's Grandma." Both kids shrieked and clung tighter to Bob.

Mom laughed. "It's okay." And I thought she looked sort of relieved.

"But here's Jonah. You love Jonah." Diane pried Cooper out of Bob's arms and handed him to me. He weighed a ton. Bob set Tucker down on the floor. "Take Jonah upstairs and show him your new toys," Diane said. She smiled at Mom and Bob. "Doug's in the kitchen." They all left.

I looked around for Liz, but she'd disappeared. Tucker was standing in front of me, with his hands on his hips. "I don't love you. I hate you," he said. "You smell funny."

"Funny," Cooper said, and he bit me, right on the arm.

I dropped him on the floor, and he started to howl. "Blended families suck," I said.

"Jonah said a bad word!" Tucker screamed.

Mom and Bob didn't talk in the car driving home, either. But I heard them talking in their room after we went to bed. It sounded like they might be arguing.

My bedroom door opening woke me up. "Jonah?" Liz whispered. I kept my eyes shut and pretended to be asleep. "Jonah?" She tapped me on the forehead. "I think I'm going to throw up."

I opened my eyes and sat up, quick. "Not in here!"

Liz was kneeling on the floor in the triangle of light from the hallway. "I really don't feel so good." She rested her forehead against the edge of the bed.

"You can't be sick in here." I shoved at her, but she didn't budge. "Go tell Mom, Liz."

She looked up at me. "You go tell her. Please?"

I thought about walking down the hall and knocking on their door. "What's wrong, exactly?"

"My stomach hurts." She patted it, like I didn't know where her stomach was.

I sat up. "Go drink some of that pink stuff in the medicine cabinet."

She made a face. "That would really make me barf. And

I don't know how much to take." She leaned forward again, so I couldn't see her face. "Do you think Mom and Bob are going to get a divorce?"

"What?"

"They were fighting, you know."

"I don't think anybody gets divorced over a salad, Liz."

"But they might." She sat back on her heels. "Do you think Mom and Dad would get married again?"

"Dad's married to Maureen, Liz."

"I know that." She rested her chin on the edge of the mattress. "But I was thinking, if Mom and Bob got divorced, and Dad and Maureen got divorced, then Mom and Dad could get married again."

I shoved at her head, but gently this time. "I thought you liked Bob. You used to like him a lot."

"It's different when he's here all the time." She picked at a tuft in my bedspread. "He yelled at me. In the car."

I thought about telling her it was her fault for spitting in my ear in the first place, but I didn't. "He's sort of a professional yeller, Liz. It's what he does for a living."

"Well, I don't like it." She pulled hard on the tuft, and some of it came loose. "And I hate cheese on my popcorn. I'll probably never have normal popcorn again in my whole life. Or get to watch *The Simpsons.*"

There was a rustle in the hallway, and Bob appeared in the door. He was wearing pajamas and slippers and a bathrobe. He looked like somebody in one of those old TV shows from the 70s. "Is something wrong?" he whispered.

"No." Liz jumped up. "I'm all better. I'm just fine." She pushed past Bob and went across the hall to her room.

Bob looked at me. "She had a stomachache," I said, "but I guess it got better."

He nodded. "Well, good night." He shut my door. But he didn't go back to the bedroom. I heard him go on down the hall and down to the living room, and then I heard the little *ding* of the computer being turned on.

He and Liz had both forgotten to turn off the hall light. I lay in bed for a while, looking at the bright outline around my door. Finally I got up and turned the light off myself.

Earthquake!

There was a note in my locker before lunch on Monday. It was folded like a paper airplane. Inside there was a big "S," and alongside it the words "murfs mile exy o mile murf tyle" were written one on top of the other, in different colored ink. It took me a minute to figure out how to read it. Then I laughed. I was pretty sure it was the same handwriting as the first two notes. And I was positive that this one wasn't from Travis and Jerry or any other guy. I thought about showing it to Amanda. Amanda was good at figuring this kind of stuff out. I jammed it into my pocket and headed for lunch.

The cafeteria was almost full when I got there. Practically the only empty seats were with Kevin and Eric.

I got my lunch and sat down across from them. Maybe

Amanda would show up with Katherine. "Hey, Jonah." Kevin had bought his lunch. He was picking the lettuce out of his taco.

"Hey, Kevin. Eric."

"So you defeated Zanbu with a spider spell?" Eric had brought his lunch from home. He had it spread out in front of him, all in little bags, probably in alphabetical order. But he wasn't eating. He was taking notes in a little blue notebook. I looked at Kevin and made a face, but Kevin acted like he didn't even notice.

"Actually, I used a tarantula spell," Kevin said. "I really didn't think it was going to work."

"Well, a spider spell got me to level six," Eric said. He was wearing a T-shirt that said, PREPARE TO BE ASSIMILATED.

I took a bite of my taco. Little shards of tortilla sprayed out of my mouth. "We got a computer," I said.

"It's about time," Kevin said.

"What kind?" Eric asked.

I didn't know what kind it was. It was gray and white.

Kevin put his hands together like he was praying. "Say you're not a Mac weenie, Jonah."

"Hey!" Eric folded his arms across his chest. "Macs rule!"

"Macs suck," Kevin said.

I thought this conversation sucked. I was sorry I'd brought the whole thing up.

"Hey, there." Travis plopped down into the empty chair beside me, and Jerry sat down in the one next to him. Eric scooted his chair back a little.

Travis put a Coke, two Ding-Dongs, and a chocolate bar on the table. "Nice lunch," I said.

Travis grinned. "I got it from those sixth-graders."

Two tables over, three sixth-grade boys were watching us. When Travis pointed his finger at them, they all looked away, fast. Jerry laughed and snagged one of the Ding-Dongs.

Behind the sixth-graders, I saw Amanda, and I thought about the note. But Katherine was with her. While I was trying to decide if I should wave, they sat down at a table with Jill and Thuy and Melanie.

Eric was gulping down his orange drink like he was afraid Travis was going to take it away from him.

"Hey, Eh-wick," Travis said. "You shouldn't drink that stuff." He took a big bite of the chocolate bar.

"Why not?" Eric asked suspiciously.

"Yellow dye number five," Travis said. He shook his head. "Very bad stuff." Jerry snorted.

79

Eric was turning the bottle, looking for the list of ingredients.

"What's it do to you?" Kevin asked.

"It ruins your love life."

"Shrinks it," Jerry said, and he laughed. He hadn't completely swallowed the Ding-Dong.

"Shrinks what?" Eric said.

I laughed. "Eric, you're such a moron."

Kevin gave me a dirty look, but I ignored him.

"Hi, guys." Sylvie and Emma came up behind me.

"How's it going?" Emma leaned over the back of my chair. The front of her body squished against my back. She rested her chin on the top of my head. "Look. We're a totem pole."

Travis and Jerry laughed.

Eric and Kevin were grabbing their stuff. "We really gotta go," Kevin said. "We have time on the computer," Eric said. They took off.

Emma and Sylvie sat down in the empty chairs. "So," Sylvie said, "what were you guys talking about?"

"Nutrition," Travis said, and Jerry and I cracked up.

"I bet," Emma said.

Jerry pointed at Sylvie's lunch bag. "You gonna eat that?"

"No." Sylvie tossed the bag on the table. "My mother makes me a sandwich every day. She knows I only eat plain yogurt and carrot sticks."

"Gross," Emma and I said together, and we both laughed.

The fire alarm went off. Not the usual long, continuous ring, but a series of short, loud buzzes.

"Earthquake drill!" Jerry shouted. "All right!"

We all piled off our chairs and crawled under the table. "Girls in the middle," Travis said.

"Why?" Jerry said.

"Safety," I said, and Sylvie and Emma giggled.

"I brought the cookies." Travis handed around the Oreos from Sylvie's lunch.

A few feet away, Brandon Ziegler was trying to stuff himself under one of the chairs.

"It'll never work, Ziggy," Jerry said.

"Manning told me to. The tables are all taken." Brandon got his head under the chair. The rest of his body stuck out into the room. We all laughed.

"You know what I heard about Brandon and Jennifer?" Sylvie asked.

"What?" Emma asked.

"In the bushes?" Sylvie said. "Behind the track?"

81

"When?" Travis asked.

"Friday," Sylvie said. "During third period. Thuy told me."

"I thought Brandon was going out with Carly," Emma said. "Jill said they were."

"I hear talking!" Mrs. Manning yelled. "It has to be totally quiet!"

Emma shuffled over so she was leaning hard against me. "If it really was an earthquake," she whispered, "wouldn't stuff be falling down, and wouldn't it be totally noisy?"

I laughed. I moved over a little, thinking I should make room for her. But she moved with me, and her body stayed pressed up against my side.

"Whose hand is that?" Sylvie said.

"Where?" Travis said.

"You know where."

"Jonah," Travis said. "Take your hands off Sylvie."

"It's not me," I said. "Must be Jerry."

"Jerry!" Sylvie said. "Oh, yuck!" She shoved Jerry. He shoved her back. She bumped into Emma. Emma sort of sprawled against me.

"Hey!" I said. I shoved Emma back toward Travis. She was laughing so hard she couldn't make any sound. Travis shoved her back at me. I lost my balance and rolled out from under the table, right into Mrs. Manning's feet.

She grabbed the collar of my shirt and pulled me up. The all-clear signal sounded on the intercom. Kids were climbing out from under tables and chairs all over the room. Amanda and Katherine were looking over at us.

Mrs. Manning watched Travis get up. "I've had just about enough nonsense from you, Travis." She jerked me back and forth by the collar.

Travis shrugged and spread his hands. "I wasn't doing anything," he said. Emma and Sylvie were standing behind him, staring at the floor. Jerry had disappeared.

"You are constantly causing a disruption," Mrs. Manning said. She pulled on my shirt one more time, then let me go.

"It wasn't his fault, Mrs. Manning," I said.

"Well, maybe an afternoon in detention writing out the earthquake safety precautions will have some impact."

"It wasn't his fault," I said again, a little louder. "It was crowded, and I slipped out." I looked under the table and then back up at her. I frowned and shook my head. "I think, you know, they waxed the floor last night, and it was just too crowded, and I just slipped." I put my hands on my hips and looked around the room. "I think we need more tables in this cafeteria. And maybe they shouldn't wax the floors so often."

"Somebody should mention it to the principal," Travis said.

I nodded. "Somebody should."

Mrs. Manning looked from me to Travis and back at me. "Earthquake drills are not a joking matter, Jonah."

"No, Mrs. Manning. They are not."

She pointed at Travis. "This is a warning. Next time I'll have to put you in detention." She paused and looked around at Emma and Sylvie and me. "All of you in detention." She pointed at Travis again. "No more nonsense." She walked off to yell at somebody else.

Emma sighed and rolled her eyes. "Close one," she said.

"My mother would kill me if I got detention," Sylvie said. She looked at Travis and me. "You guys were great."

Travis put his arm around my shoulder. "We are, aren't we?"

I punched him in the ribs. "Good risk-taking," I said.

"Good energy," Sylvie and Emma said at the same time.

"Travis!" Tiffany waved from across the room. "See you later," Travis said, and he took off.

The bell rang for next period. "We gotta go," Sylvie said. She started off between the tables.

Emma looked at me. "I have a really important question for you."

"What's that?"

"How do Smurfs smile?"

I grinned. "Smurfs smile sexy."

"Emma!" Sylvie shouted. "We're going to be *so* late."

"I'm coming," Emma said. "What a nag." She gave me a grin. "See you in drama."

"Yes!" I shouted as soon as they were out the door. I dug the note out of my pocket and read it again. I'd known it. I'd known all along that Emma was the one sending those notes to me. And I liked Emma. She was cute and funny. We were almost exactly the same height. And, best of all, I had it in writing that she wanted to go out with me. "Yes!" I said again. This was perfect.

"Jonah?"

Katherine had come up behind me. "Hi there." I knew I was still grinning.

"Hi." She glanced back, and I saw Amanda give her a thumbs-up just before she disappeared through the cafeteria door. Katherine took a deep breath and stared down at the floor. "Look. I have to ask you this now, because if I think about it, I'll never ask you." She stopped.

I knew what she was going to say, and I wanted to say, "No. Wait. Stop."

But she took another deep breath and went on, fast. "I was wondering if you'd want to go out with me."

I stared at her.

She looked up at me. She was at least two inches shorter than me. "I mean, I wouldn't just ask you, but Amanda said she thought . . . Amanda said *you* were going to ask me, and then you didn't . . ." She bent down all of a sudden and picked up a potato-chip bag somebody had dropped. "Unless Amanda was wrong."

"No," I said. "No. See. I *was* going to ask you. I mean, I was getting around to it."

She crumpled up the bag. "It's okay if you don't want to. Go out with me. I mean, I totally understand. And I think we can still be friends. Or maybe we could start being friends. Because I do like you." The bag was a tight ball in her fist.

I stuffed Emma's note back into my pocket. "I do want to go out with you."

"You mean it? You're not just saying it?" She did have a nice smile.

"I mean it. I'm not just saying it. I really want to go out with you." She was still smiling at me, like I was supposed to do something. Hug her. Or kiss her. I reached out and punched her on the shoulder.

"Ow!" She rubbed at her arm, but she was still smiling. Behind us, the custodians were starting to sweep the floor. "Look. I've gotta go." She punched me back, just a tap on the shoulder. "This is so cool. I mean, I'm really glad."

"Yeah," I said. "Yeah, I'm glad, too."

She jogged across the cafeteria, her ponytail swinging back and forth behind her. It was really great hair.

"Jonah." Bob was standing behind me. He pointed to the clock. "You're late for Spanish. Is something wrong?"

I shook my head. "No. No. Everything's just terrific."

The Golden Jockstrap

There was another note in my locker first thing the next day. I thought it might be from Emma, but it wasn't. It said, "Dear Jonah. Even though I don't know you that well, I'm really, really glad that we're going out together." It was signed, "Love, Katherine." The ink was only one color. There were no funny pictures.

Katherine stopped by my desk when science ended. Emma had already left. "I'll walk you to social studies," Katherine said.

"How do you know what I have next?"

She'd done something different with her makeup, and her eyes looked very big and wide. "Amanda told me your whole schedule."

Across the room, Amanda was grinning at us.

"I know you were late for Spanish yesterday," Katherine

said. "We'd better get going." As we walked out into the hall, she reached out and slid her hand into mine.

Besides Liz, I had never actually held hands with a girl. Katherine's felt small and warm, and I tried to be careful not to hold it too tight. She squeezed my hand and smiled, kind of a funny smile. Maybe I was holding her hand *too* gently. Maybe she thought I didn't really want to hold her hand. I tightened my grip. "Ouch," she said. I loosened my grip, but she kept hanging on. I decided to just leave my hand in hers.

At the door to Spurl's room, she turned to me. "I'll meet you right here when class is over so I can walk you to math."

"Okay," I said. Although I felt kind of funny. I mean, I could get to my classes by myself.

She wagged her finger at me. "We don't want you to be late again."

Jerry had come up behind me. He watched Katherine walk down the hall. "Are you two going out?" he asked finally.

I took a deep breath. "Yeah," I said. "Yeah, we are."

"Great hair," he said. Then he shook his head. "But she sort of talks like my mother."

Katherine walked me to all my classes. She gave me the

apple out of her lunch, because she was afraid I hadn't gotten enough to eat. And she reminded me three times that I had a Spanish test on Thursday.

All day, I dreaded facing Emma. I didn't see her until drama club. Katherine had met me at my locker, and we walked in together, with Katherine holding my hand. Emma and Sylvie were in the corner, talking. Emma looked up at me and Katherine. And then she turned back to Sylvie and went on talking like nothing was wrong or different. Sylvie said something, and Emma laughed. She didn't even look like she cared, and it made me sort of mad.

"Hey, Jonah!" Travis was lying with his head in Tiffany's lap. "Over here."

But Katherine tugged on my hand. "Let's sit with Amanda and Kevin." And she led me over to the other side of the room.

The phone rang that night, and Liz got it before I could. "It's a girl!" she yelled. "For Jonah!"

I took it in the bedroom.

"Hi! This is Katherine."

"I know," I said. "Hi."

She sighed. "Listen. Is it okay I'm calling you? Because my mother said it might not be."

"No, no. It's fine." I hoped she hadn't heard Liz.

She sighed again. "My mother worries about the dumbest things. It's so embarrassing sometimes."

"Yeah, well, my mother married the principal," I said. "Now that's embarrassing."

Katherine laughed and laughed. It made me feel good.

"You're so funny, Jonah," she said. "It's one of the things I like best about you."

"Well," I said, and I tried to think of the thing I liked best about her, but all I could think of was her hair, how it was so long and smooth, and the fact that she was shorter than me. "I like you, too," I said, finally.

"Look, the reason I called," she said, "is I just talked to Amanda. And, I mean, seeing as how we're going out together, I think we should do things together."

"You and Amanda?" I said.

"No." She sounded a little ticked. "You and me, Jonah. That's the way it works when people are going out together. They go out together."

"Okay." I looked at myself in the mirror on the back on the door. I had a zit forming right in the middle of my forehead. "So like, you mean, going out going out?"

"On a date," she said.

"You mean a *date* date." I didn't know why I was saying

everything twice, but it was starting to make me nervous. "You and me."

"Well, and Kevin and Amanda. My mom won't let me go out on single dates until I'm sixteen."

"Oh." I wondered if she'd told her mother about us. And, if we went out on a date, even one with Amanda and Kevin, I'd have to tell *my* mother. And Liz would find out about it, because everybody in this family always found out everything. I could hear her screaming, "Jonah has a girlfriend! Jonah has a girlfriend!"

"Are you still there?" Katherine asked.

"Yeah. Yeah, I'm here." I'd twisted the phone cord around my finger so hard my finger was turning red. "What would we do exactly?" I closed my eyes. I couldn't believe I'd just said that. "I mean, *where* would we go?"

"Amanda and I are going to plan it all out. Amanda's really excited about it. It'll be a lot of fun. Don't you think it sounds like fun?"

I didn't know if she meant the planning or the actual date. "Oh, yeah," I said. "It sounds just perfect."

There were two notes from Katherine in my locker on Wednesday. The first one was about the date. It was two pages, single spaced, and it was mostly about how much

Katherine hated horror movies and why she wouldn't go see one even if Kevin wanted to. I didn't have time to read the whole thing. The second note was to remind me about the Spanish test.

In drama, Ms. Landau said, "Today we're going to start something a little different. You're going to start to use some of the things you've been learning—"

"We've been learning something?" Travis said.

Ms. Landau ignored him. "To put on some skits." She smiled around at us. "We're going to start with fairy tales, because I know you're all familiar with the stories. I've divided you into groups . . ." She kept talking over the shouts of "No fair!" and the loud, pained groans. ". . . and I've assigned each group a fairy tale."

I ended up in a group with Katherine, Melanie, Amanda, a seventh-grader named Cathy Maciariello, and Travis. Our fairy tale was *Cinderella*.

"The first thing you need to do," Ms. Landau said, "is work out a script. Pick a place to work. Here in the drama room or out in the cafeteria. You can even sit in the front foyer."

"Let's go out in the foyer," Travis said.

We picked a spot by the front door, and Amanda and

Melanie immediately got into an argument over who was going to get to write the script. Amanda really liked to write stuff.

"Katherine'll have to be one of the mice," Travis said.

"Why?" Katherine said.

"Because you're so little." Travis laughed, and he picked her up and swung her around.

"We don't have to have mice," Amanda said.

"Of course we do," Melanie said.

I wandered over to the big display case in the corner. It was full of pictures of sixth-graders picking up garbage along the Willamette. They all looked really young and happy. I couldn't even remember sixth grade. It seemed like a long, long time ago.

There was a burst of laughter through the open door of the cafeteria. Emma's group was sitting there by the door. They were all cracking up about something. They looked like they were having a really good time.

"What do you think, Jonah?" Katherine grabbed my hand and pulled me back over to our group.

"About what?"

"Travis says *The Hunchback of Notre Dame* was the best Disney cartoon."

"That Esmeralda," Travis said. "She's got big—"

"Travis!" Katherine said. "You are so gross."

"I liked *The Lion King* best," Cathy Maciariello said. Travis and Katherine groaned and rolled their eyes. Cathy ignored them. "Watch this." And she did a perfect cartwheel, right in the middle of the foyer.

"Seventh-graders," Travis and Katherine said simultaneously. But I thought it was sort of cool. I couldn't do a cartwheel.

"There don't have to be mice in *Cinderella*, Melanie," Amanda shouted.

The next day, Ms. Landau said she thought all the groups should work at tables in the cafeteria. "I'm afraid some people are abusing their privileges," she said. She sounded surprised.

When we were all seated around one of the tables, Melanie plunked down a stack of paper. "Look," she said, "I've written out the whole script." Amanda opened her mouth, but Melanie went right on talking. "*And* I've assigned the parts. I'm Cinderella, because I have this great dress. And Jonah's the prince."

"I don't want to be the prince," I said.

"*I* have a great dress," Cathy Maciariello said. "Why can't I be Cinderella?"

"I think Jonah should be Cinderella," Travis said.

95

We all looked at him. Then everybody laughed, except me and Melanie. "Look," Melanie started.

"You know, it's not such a bad idea," Amanda said. She had that serious, thoughtful look on her face that made everybody listen to her. "I think Jonah *should* be Cinderella."

"What?" I said.

"It would be funny," Amanda said. She looked around the table. "Everybody knows the story already, and if we just do it, it'll be . . ."

"Boring," Cathy said. She was reading the script over Melanie's shoulder. "Really boring."

"Besides," Travis said, "there aren't enough guy parts."

"But I wrote it all out," Melanie said. She looked like she was going to cry.

"We can still use it," Amanda said. "We'll just change the people a little. Jonah can be the Cinderella person."

"Cinderelvis," Cathy said.

"Yes!" Amanda said. "And Travis could be the fairy godfather."

"Travis could be the straight godfather, thank you very much," Travis said.

"Like the guy in the movie," Katherine said.

"Marlon Brando," Travis said. "It's a great movie."

96

"I've seen it four times," Katherine said. She looked at me. "Have you ever seen it, Jonah? I can lend you our copy."

I'd watched the beginning at Kevin's one time. We'd turned it off, because it was totally confusing and sort of boring. "I don't want to be Cinderella," I said.

"Cinder*elvis*," Cathy said.

"We'll have to change everything," Melanie said. "I mean, does he have ugly stepbrothers instead of stepsisters?"

"I'd like to be a guy," Cathy said. "It'll be fun."

"But you're not a guy," Melanie said, like Cathy was being really stupid.

"We might as well practice," Amanda said. "Some of us are going to have to be guys in *Romeo and Juliet.*"

"So do we change the wicked stepmother to a stepfather?" Katherine asked. She'd pulled the script away from Melanie and was writing notes in the margin.

"Jonah already has a wicked stepfather," Travis said.

"Ha-ha. Very funny," I said.

"Let's leave it a stepmother," Amanda said, and Katherine made a note on the script.

"Look." Melanie grabbed the script back. "It's just not going to work. You're not thinking this through. I mean, what does this Cinderelvis drop for the prince . . . princess . . . whoever to find? A guitar?"

"I don't have a guitar," I said.

"Maybe a sneaker?" Amanda said.

"Too obvious," Travis said.

"A blue suede shoe?" Katherine said.

"I don't have any blue suede shoes, either," I said. "I don't have any blue shoes at all."

So?" Melanie said. "What can he drop?" She sounded like she thought she was winning.

"A jockstrap," Travis said.

Nobody said anything. And then Cathy and Amanda and Katherine burst out laughing.

"Perfect!" Katherine said, clapping her hands.

"What does a jockstrap have to do with Elvis?" Melanie said.

"Nothing," Travis said. "It's funnier that way." He looked at me. "You have one of those, don't you?"

"Of course," I lied. The last sport I'd played had been indoor soccer in fifth grade, and they hadn't made us wear them.

"You know what would be even better?" Amanda said. "If it was a golden jockstrap. I think Elvis would have a golden one."

"Thank you very much, Amanda," I said, and they all laughed, except Melanie. She groaned and put her head on the table.

"Could you paint your jockstrap gold, Jonah?" Amanda asked.

"Oh, sure. Absolutely. Why not?"

Amanda grabbed the script back, and she started writing down ideas. Travis and Cathy made suggestions. Melanie sulked.

Katherine leaned over and put her arm around my shoulder. "This is going to be so great. Don't you think it's going to be great, Jonah?"

For some reason, her arm around me made me feel a little better. I sort of leaned up against her, and I slid my arm around her waist.

I saw Bob watching us from the door of the cafeteria. I wiggled out from under Katherine's arm and picked up a page of the script. "So," I said in a loud voice, "where are the mice?"

So Complicated

On Saturday, I played hockey again with Travis and Jerry. I kept waiting for Travis to make some dumb joke about jockstraps, which I knew Jerry would absolutely love, but he didn't.

We were taking turns teeing up and taking slapshots when Tiffany rode up on her bike. "Hey, Travis," she said.

Travis dropped his stick and skated over to talk to her.

Jerry nudged me. "Watch this. They French kiss, you know."

"Everybody knows that, Jerry," I said.

But Travis and Tiffany didn't start kissing. They didn't even touch each other. They talked for a couple of minutes, and then Tiffany rode off up the sidewalk.

Travis skated back over and picked up his stick.

"What was that all about?" Jerry asked.

Travis shrugged. He hooked the ball and shot it toward the water bottles. "We broke up."

Jerry and I looked at each other. "Just like that?" I asked. "I mean, just now?"

"It's been coming for a while." Travis skated after the ball.

"I thought you guys were pretty tight," Jerry said.

"It got boring," Travis said. He snagged the ball and dribbled it back toward us. He stopped a few feet away. "I'm sort of interested in somebody else, anyway."

Jerry looked at me. "I think she dumped him."

Travis shot the ball, hard, and it hit Jerry right in the stomach. "Ow!" he shouted, and he doubled up, moaning.

"I told you. We've been talking about it for a while." Travis skated back over beside us.

Jerry stood up, rubbing his middle. "So," he said, "do you think Tiffany'd go out with me?"

Travis laughed—a really loud, obnoxious laugh. But Jerry wasn't laughing. And I realized I'd never thought about Jerry going out with anybody.

"Maybe, Jer," I said.

"In your dreams," Travis said, and he passed me the ball. "Take a shot, Truman."

My Mom Married the PRINCIPAL

Mom and Liz were arguing in the kitchen when I got home.

"I don't want to be an astronaut for Halloween," Liz said. "I have to be a cat. Stephanie and Angie and Karen are all being cats."

Mom sighed. "Libby. Two weeks ago you wanted to be an astronaut. We already bought the costume. I am not buying another costume now."

Liz stomped out of the kitchen. Mom looked at me. "Do you need me to buy something, too?"

Yes, Mom, I thought. I need you to buy me a jockstrap. A golden one. But I couldn't say it.

On Sunday we hiked up Saddle Mountain. Mom and Bob held hands the whole way. Liz walked way ahead of all of us.

Katherine was waiting for me at my locker Monday morning. She took my hand and swung it back and forth. "We finally got it worked out."

"What?"

"The date!" She frowned at me. "You haven't forgotten, have you?"

"No, I haven't forgotten." We started walking down the hall. I kept watch for Bob.

"Amanda and I were on the phone for hours yesterday."

"What did you work out?"

"Well, we thought about a movie, but there are no good ones showing. And I said bowling—"

"Not bowling," I said.

"That's what Amanda said, too." She smiled and swung my hand harder. "So we finally decided on laser-tag. And Kevin said it was fine with him."

"Okay," I said. Laser-tag was fine with me, too, although I wondered why they'd asked Kevin first and not me.

"Not this Friday, because Kevin's grounded," Katherine said.

It used to be that I knew stuff like that about Kevin first. "He's grounded?"

"Yes. He erased his brother's name off the high scores of some game, and his mom got really mad."

I nodded. That sounded like Kevin's mom.

"So laser-tag a week from Friday. And you don't have to put it on your calendar or anything, because I'll remind you."

I bet she'd remind me. "Okay," I said. Now I was just going to have to figure out how I was going to tell Mom about it.

In drama, Ms. Landau said we should have our scripts

ready, and we should start working on rehearsing the skits. "We'll perform them next week," she said, and she laughed when we all groaned.

Amanda had actually already rewritten the whole play, and I had to admit it was pretty funny. "We have to decide who gets what part," Melanie said when our group met back in the cafeteria.

"Well, Jonah's Cinderelvis and Travis is the Godfather," Katherine said. "Cathy, do you still want to be an ugly stepbrother?" Cathy nodded.

"I'll be the other one," Amanda said. "I gave them some great lines."

"And I'm the princess," Melanie said. "Because I have the dress."

Amanda and Katherine looked at each other. "So Katherine's the wicked stepmother?" Amanda said.

Travis snorted. "That doesn't work. Nobody's going to believe she's a wicked anything."

"Katherine should be the princess," Cathy said.

"I have the dress," Melanie said.

"But look." Cathy pointed to the script. "Cinderelvis and the Princess kiss in the last scene here. Are you going to kiss Jonah?"

Melanie and I looked at each other.

"The stepmother is a way bigger part," Amanda said. "And you can be the director, too."

"Well," Melanie said. "I guess." She frowned at Katherine. "My dress won't fit you."

"We can pin it," Amanda said.

Katherine mouthed "thank you" across the table to Amanda, and Amanda grinned. Katherine squeezed my hand, and I smiled, too, although I was wondering why Melanie hadn't wanted to kiss me. I mean, no way did I want to kiss her, but why didn't she want to kiss me?

We worked on the skit all that week. I had to admit that Melanie was a pretty good director. On Wednesday, Ms. Landau made Emma's group go work alone in the classroom because they couldn't stop laughing about something. "You guys are just having too much fun," Ms. Landau said.

Liz was on the phone when I got home on Friday. "It's Dad," she said, holding out the receiver. I hated it when she got him first. She always told him everything good. He asked about school and how my math class was going. He said he was really glad I was playing roller-hockey. "I'll tell Maureen you're using the skates," he said. I thought about telling him that I needed a jockstrap, but somehow it seemed like a lot to explain on the phone.

After I hung up, I went outside and put on my skates and practiced wrist shots. Dead leaves had piled up along the garage door, and, if I hit the ball just right, I could make them fly up, like a leaf explosion.

"Hey, there." Amanda came across from her yard. She was wearing jeans and a big fleece jacket with penguins on it.

I snapped the ball hard, and it banged against the door.

"You're getting pretty good at that."

I skated around her and hooked the ball. Then I dribbled it down the driveway. I shot from the end, but the ball hopped on a piece of gravel and rolled into the grass.

Amanda picked it up. "I need to talk to you."

"Okay." I skated over to the porch steps and sat down. The cement was cold and damp through my jeans.

Amanda sat down beside me. "It's this date thing." She rolled the ball between her hands. "This is so complicated. Who's idea was this, anyway?"

"Katherine said you really wanted to do it."

She looked at me. "She told me you really wanted to do it."

"I do want to do it." And I did. I just didn't want to have to worry about it so much before it even happened. And I didn't want to talk to my mother about it. "So what's the problem?"

"My mother."

"*Your* mother?"

Amanda flopped down on the grass. Then she sat back up. "Katherine and I have spent so much time trying to work all this out. I mean, we've gone over and over about fifty different ideas and times before we settled on this laser-tag thing. We were on the phone all the time. It was driving me nuts. And then my mother says I can't go out on a date until I'm sixteen."

"I thought that was the single date thing," I said.

"That's Katherine's mother. My mother says the only way I can go is if there's a group. A big group."

There was a weed growing up out of the edge of the driveway. I poked it with my stick. "So how many people are we talking about?"

"At least six kids have to go. It's like she has a rule book or something. And you would not believe how hard it is to find six people who can all do something on the same night." She wrapped her arms around her knees. "First Kevin gets grounded, the idiot. Then I was going to ask Tawana, but in P.E. on Wednesday she told Amelia that

Katherine is too skinny, and Amelia told Jen and Jen told Katherine today in English. I don't think Katherine's speaking to Amelia or Jen, and she's definitely not speaking to Tawana. So I may try Jill or maybe Thuy." Amanda sighed, like she'd run out of steam. She put her head on her knees and looked at me, sort of sideways. "Katherine still wants to do it. And Kevin said it was okay with him. Is it okay with you?"

Actually, it wasn't okay with me. I thought going with a whole bunch of kids sounded dumb. I thought it sounded like something Liz and her friends would do. But how could I say no when they'd all said they wanted to do it? "Sure," I said. "Sure. It's okay with me."

Amanda sat up and threw her arms around me. She felt very soft and squishy and warm. "You're such a good sport, Jonah. I know exactly why Katherine likes you." She let go of me and tossed the ball up in the air and caught it. "You're a cute couple. I mean, you look like you go together."

"That's good," I said.

She tossed the ball again. "Speaking of couples, did you hear that Travis dumped Tiffany?"

I shook my head. Then I nodded. "Yeah, I heard. Only it wasn't him. It was a mutual dumping."

Amanda shrugged. "Jill told me Tiffany was really crushed."

"She didn't look crushed. And I think two people can break up if it's boring, and they don't even really like each other. I mean, just because everybody else thinks they should be going out together, doesn't mean they should be." Or just because they look like they should be going out.

Amanda was leaning back again, frowning at me. "Do you like Tiffany or something?"

"No. I don't like Tiffany."

"Just thought I'd check." She leaned close to me again. "You want to know the other big piece of gossip?"

I sort of wanted to go back to my wrist shots, but I said, "Sure."

"Sylvie says that Emma's totally bummed because she really liked this guy, and she was going to ask him to go out with her, only he started going out with somebody else. We had a sub in English today, and we spent the whole class trying to figure out who it could have been. Do you have any ideas?"

I shook my head. Emma was bummed? I'd thought she didn't care. I thought she hadn't even noticed I was going out with Katherine. I started to grin.

"Plus," Amanda said, "Sylvie says the guy knew Emma liked him and wanted to go out with him, and he just blew her off."

I stopped grinning and stood up. "I'm too cold. I gotta move around." I hadn't blown her off. If she'd signed the stupid notes in the first place . . .

Amanda stood up, too. "Well, I'm glad this date thing is going to work out. It'll be good for you and Katherine to do something together. Get to know each other better."

I nodded.

"Aren't you going to thank me?" She tapped me in the chest with the ball, and I rolled backward a little on my skates.

"Thank you for what?"

"If it hadn't been for me, you guys wouldn't even be together. You'd still be trying to figure out how to ask each other to go out."

She tossed the ball down onto the pavement, and I stopped it with my stick. I nodded my head slowly. "That's right. Thanks, Amanda," I said. I slammed the ball against the door. "Thanks a lot."

Easier Than I Expected

Mom was in the kitchen rinsing dishes when I went inside.

I realized she was actually all alone. I could explain the whole date thing. I could ask her for a ride to the laser-tag place. And maybe even for a jockstrap.

Liz stomped into the kitchen. "I hate that computer! I died on level four!"

"At least it's working again," I said.

"Maybe Bob can help you when he gets home," Mom said.

Liz jerked out one of the chairs and sat down. I could tell she wasn't going to go anywhere anytime soon. "Where is Bob?" I asked.

"He had a meeting. Dinner's going to be a little late."

"What is for dinner?"

"Pizza." Mom smiled at me. "It's an old family favorite."

"Great," I said.

"But not with mushrooms," Liz said. "I hate mushrooms."

Mom clinked a glass against a bowl. "Bob likes mushrooms, Libby."

"You can pick them off," I said.

"They leave dents. I hate pizza with dents."

"You're such a baby."

"You're an idiot."

"Libby," Mom said, "there's a glass in the living room by the computer. Go get it, okay?"

"Make Jonah do it. He never does anything around here."

"Oh, yeah. Right," I said.

"Liz." Mom was staring down into the sink, her hands braced on the edge of the counter. "Just do it."

"I have to do *everything* around here," Liz said. But she went to get the glass.

I sat down in her chair. "What's wrong with her?"

Mom was wiping her hands on a towel. "She's just having a hard time right now. I think fourth grade is kind of stressful."

I snorted. "Wait until she gets to eighth grade."

Liz came back in and clanked the glass down in the sink. It was the glass I'd left in there the night before, but I decided not to mention it. "I bet if I ask Bob, he'd buy me a cat costume."

Mom put her hands on her hips. "Elizabeth Amy Truman. Don't you dare ask Bob." She looked at me. "He's bought enough things for you two."

"I didn't ask him to buy me anything," I said. "Not lately."

"You got a stick," Liz said, "and a hockey net."

"That's different," I said. "I needed those. You don't need a cat costume."

"The point is," Mom said, "you could treat him like something more than a walking wallet."

"He likes to buy stuff for us," Liz said. I actually thought that was true, too, and I nodded. "I bet he'd *like* to buy me a cat costume," Liz added.

"I don't care what Bob likes," Mom said.

The door opened, and Bob walked in. "The meeting got canceled," he said. He raised his eyebrows at Mom. "Am I interrupting something?"

On Monday morning, Mrs. Manning threw Travis out of science for saying something rude to Katherine. I was

113

watching Emma work on the computer with Kevin, and I sort of missed the whole thing.

"What was that about?" I asked when Katherine was walking me to Spurl's class.

She shrugged. "Mrs. Manning overreacts sometimes." She squeezed my hand. "Did you remember to study for your math test?"

Travis walked in halfway through social studies. He'd grabbed a box of paperclips from a desk in the office, and we spent the rest of the period shooting them at Thuy and Jill.

In drama we acted out the whole Cinderelvis thing. Amanda and Cathy really got into being guys. Cathy kept pretending to spit, and Amanda was scratching under her arms, until Melanie told her it was disgusting.

Ms. Landau stopped by and watched us work. Travis and I were doing the godfather part. Ms. Landau laughed when we were done and said, "Good energy. Is Cinderelvis going to drop his sneaker for the princess to find?"

We all looked at each other. "Sort of," Amanda said, finally.

"Sounds like fun," Ms. Landau said. She clapped her hands. "Okay, everybody. Let's meet all together up on the stage!"

When we were finally all together, Ms. Landau had us sit in a big circle. She handed out blue booklets. "This is *A Young Performer's Romeo and Juliet*," she said, like maybe some of us couldn't read the cover. "We're going to read through the play, just going around the circle, taking turns. No acting," she added, looking at Melanie.

When we were done, all the girls sighed, and Thuy said, "That is *so* sad."

Ms. Landau clapped her hands. "For the rest of this week, we'll spend the first part of the session working on our fairy tales. Then we'll do readings of some of the scenes from the play." She grinned her lots-of-teeth grin. "I'm going to start making some casting decisions based on the readings and your work in these skits."

We did *Romeo and Juliet* scenes for the rest of that day. I got to be Romeo twice, Tybalt once, and Juliet's father once.

When we were done, Jill asked if the costumes were here yet. "Not yet," Ms. Landau said.

Tiffany raised her hand. "If some of the girls have to take guy parts, do we have to wear guy costumes?"

"I'm afraid so," Ms. Landau said.

There were moans and groans. But Melanie said, "I'd like to be Romeo."

There were *lots* of moans and groans. "Jonah's going to be Romeo," Thuy said, and just about everybody nodded.

Ms. Landau laughed. "Let's just say that Romeo will definitely be a boy."

On Tuesday, Travis and I finished up the box of paper-clips in social studies, and on Wednesday, Spurl made me move seats. "I want you to sit with Melanie and Eric, Jonah," he said.

"But I like it where I am," I said.

He frowned at me. "This is not up for discussion. I don't know what's gotten into you lately."

I rolled my eyes, but I went and sat down in the seat next to Eric. He was reading a video-games magazine and didn't even look at me. Melanie gave me one of her smirks.

"Jonah has to sit with the nerds," Travis said.

Spurl threw him out.

Amanda grabbed Kevin and me as we were coming out of band. "Look. Have you talked to your parents about Friday night?"

"Yeah," Kevin said. "It's fine."

Amanda looked at me.

"Not yet."

"Well you'd better. My mom was talking this morning about calling all the other parents. Just to make sure everyone knows what's going on." Amanda shook her head. "So. If you don't want your mom to hear it from my mom first . . ."

"Okay. Okay."

Amanda took off for P.E. I looked at Kevin. "Do your parents know you and Amanda are going out?"

"Yeah. We went to a Beavers game in August. They figured it out."

I nodded. "Was it, like, a big deal?"

He shook his head. "My brother Mark's been dating this girl since he was in fifth grade. My mom and dad are sort of broken in."

For the first time, I wished I had an older brother. I wished Mom was broken in.

Mom had a meeting after school, and she didn't get home until almost 5:30. And then Liz said she needed help with this history project. I knew I'd never get Mom alone. So at dinner, when Bob asked me about my day, I said, "A bunch of us were thinking about playing laser-tag on Friday."

"How many's a bunch?" Mom asked.

"Six, I think. Amanda and Kevin and Jill and Katherine."

"That's five," Liz said. She put down her fork and

counted on her fingers. "You and Kevin and Amanda and Katherine Chang and Jill. That's five."

I wanted to ask her where she'd gotten Chang, but I decided I really didn't want to know. "It all depends on who can go," I said. "Amanda's organizing it." I looked at Mom. She liked Amanda.

"I suppose it's okay," Mom said, "although I'm not sure how you'll get there."

"You just drop me off. It's in the little mall over by the Costco." I suddenly had a terrible thought. "You don't have to stay or anything."

She and Bob laughed. "That's not the problem." She looked at Bob. "I have that baby shower that evening."

"I can drive him. Just so it's after five. And I can pick him up anytime."

"Okay," Mom said.

"Okay," I said. That had been way easier than I'd expected.

At lunch the next day, Amanda asked me if I'd worked everything out. "Everything's okay, Amanda," I said.

"Do you know where the laser-tag place is?" Katherine asked. "Because I can draw you a map."

"I know where it is," I said.

She smiled and took my hand, which made it sort of hard to eat my spaghetti, but I didn't say anything.

She and Amanda started talking about what they were going to wear Friday night. And Kevin and Eric were discussing an episode of *Star Trek* where somebody turns into a Borg. Across the room, I could see Sylvie and Emma and Thuy doing something with a can of Coke. They were giggling and laughing.

"See you later," Amanda said. I looked up and realized that she and Kevin and Eric were leaving.

"Where are they going?"

Katherine laughed. "To the computer lab. Where else? Poor Amanda."

Over by the door, a chair crashed onto the floor. Travis had a sixth-grader in a headlock. I shook my head. "Travis strikes again," I said.

Katherine let go of my hand. "People have been talking about you and Travis. Hanging out together, I mean."

She had a funny sort of serious, concerned look on her face. Not only did she sound like my mother, she even sort of looked like her. "He's a really good skater," I said. I tried to think of something else good about Travis. "And he's funny."

"Oh, I know." She nodded her head very seriously. "He's been great in drama. I mean, really not . . ." She blushed and shook her head. I knew she was trying hard to think of something nice to say about Travis.

Across the room, Sylvie shouted, "Oh, no!" and Emma and Thuy laughed really loud.

"You know one of the things I hate about middle school?" I said.

"What?" Katherine took my hand again.

"Everybody thinks they know everything there is to know about everybody else." Katherine looked like she was going to say something, but I just kept going. "Don't you think the whole point of this is to get to know other people? I mean, if you just hang around with the same people the whole time, well then there's a whole bunch of people you never get to know." I was thinking about Emma, but I couldn't say that. I waved my other hand to kind of include the whole cafeteria. "I mean, we're not all even going to go to the same high school. Some of these people we'll never even see again."

Katherine was nodding her head. "If you only hang out with the same people, well, you only get to know half the people," she said.

I nodded, too. "Exactly. Like I would never have gotten

to know Travis." Emma and Thuy and Sylvie were cracking up again. And I realized Emma probably didn't even care if she never got to know me. This whole conversation was getting really depressing.

Katherine looked at the clock. "Oh my gosh." She stood up. "I forgot I've got to meet Mrs. Caine before class." She smiled down at me. "You're so cool, Jonah." And she leaned over and kissed me, quick, on the cheek. Travis waved to her as she went out the door, and she smiled and waved back.

I knew she was just being nice to him to be nice to me. I started gathering up the napkins and wrappers we'd left out on the table. Katherine was a very nice girl. So why did she drive me so crazy?

"Hey, Jonah." Emma was standing beside me.

"Oh. Wow. Hi." I gave her my biggest smile.

"I have something for you." She set one of the little ranch dressing containers on the table. Only it wasn't full of ranch dressing. It was full of something wetter and darker, so full the little top bulged out.

"Wow," I said again, and I tried to think of some funny, smart remark. Only, when I looked up, she was running toward the cafeteria door.

The lid exploded off the dressing container, and Coke

sprayed out across the table. I jumped back, and my hand caught the edge of my tray. Leftover spaghetti and salad flew up onto me and all over the floor.

"Way to go, Jonah!" Travis and Jerry were sitting on one of the tables near the window. They both started to clap and cheer.

"Jonah Truman." Mrs. Manning came stomping across the room. She frowned at Travis and Jerry. Then she frowned at me. "Just what has gotten into you lately? Clean this mess up at once."

"It wasn't my fault, Mrs. Manning." I tried to look serious and sincere. "See, I was sitting here . . ."

She pointed her finger at me. "I've had enough of you and your friends, Jonah. Now clean this up." And she turned and walked away.

Just Like a Field Trip

Katherine was waiting at my locker the next morning. "I'm really excited about tonight," she said.

I was looking right into her eyes. She was the same height as me, maybe even a little taller. For a second, I had the scary feeling that maybe I'd shrunk during the night.

"The date?" she said.

"Oh. Yeah. I'm excited, too." I looked down at her feet. She was wearing black shiny boots instead of her usual sneakers. I heaved a sigh of relief.

"The thing is?" She rocked back on the heel of one boot. "It turns out I need a ride."

"A ride?"

"Yes." She shoved her hair. It was different, too. Fluffier, sort of. "My mom and dad have to go to this dumb class.

Something about living with teenagers. So I was wondering? Could I get a ride with you?"

"Uh . . ."

"It would be more like a real date then. You know, if we came in the same car?"

Unfortunately we would also be in the same car with the principal.

"I can always ask Amanda. I mean, if you think it won't be okay."

"No. No. It'll be okay. I mean, it'll be good."

"Great!" She threw her arms around me and gave me a big, tight hug. I hugged her back. She moved closer against me. I was thinking maybe I should kiss her, and I was trying to figure out how to move my head down toward her mouth without loosening my arms, when a deep voice behind us said, "No overt displays of affection in the hallway."

Katherine and I jumped apart.

"Gotcha!" Travis said. He was standing there with Jerry. They were both laughing.

"You idiot, Travis," Katherine said.

"It was just a joke," Jerry said.

"It wasn't funny." Katherine punched Travis.

"Hey!" He punched back at her, but he missed. She hit him again. Travis laughed and grabbed her and held her arms down.

"Travis," I started.

Bob came down the hallway. He frowned at all of us. "I think you people must have better things to do."

There was a note in my locker that afternoon. It had Katherine's address and phone number and a map to her house. She lived in the development over by Travis.

When I got home, it took me a long time to figure out what to wear to play laser-tag. I knew dark clothes would work best. I finally decided on my T-shirt with the Bauer logo and my new jeans. If Mom were home, she'd tell me they were too low and I should pull them up. But she wasn't home. The zit in the middle of my forehead was huge now. It looked like I had another eye. But there was nothing I could do about it.

Bob got home a little after 5:00. Liz said she wanted to come along to drop me off, but Bob said no. "We'll go out to dinner as soon as I get back. Your choice."

I got in the front seat of the car. There was an empty Coke cup and a gas-station receipt on the floor. "Oh, by the way, is it okay if we're giving somebody else a ride?"

"Certainly," Bob said. "Who? Amanda?"

I was concentrating very hard on fastening my seat belt. "No. Katherine Chang."

"Okay. Where does she live?"

I told him. He backed out of the driveway, slowly and carefully. Bob was a very slow and careful driver. He was worse than Mom.

He stopped at the stop sign on Hoodview. "You know," he said, peering out the windshield to the left, "both Genny Manning and Ron Spurl stopped by my office today."

"No kidding," I said. I was checking my wallet, making sure I had money.

Bob made the turn onto Hoodview. "They both wanted to talk to me about how they think your behavior has changed since you started hanging around with Travis." He looked away from the road and looked at me, just for a second.

"Oh," I said. I didn't know what else I was supposed to say.

"I talked to your mom," Bob said, "and—"

"You called Mom at work and told her?" I couldn't believe it.

Bob sighed. The lights from the dashboard made shadows under his eyes and mouth. "She called me, and I just mentioned it." He stopped for a red light. "I didn't feel it was my place . . ." He tapped his hand on the steering wheel and didn't finish the sentence.

The Coke cup squished under my foot. "I really need a jockstrap," I said.

"A what?"

"A jockstrap. And some gold paint." I nodded toward the light. "It's green."

He drove through the intersection. "Is this for hockey?"

"No, drama. We're doing this play. Cinderelvis? And I have to drop a golden jockstrap on the floor for the princess to find, and I don't have one." I sighed. "And I sort of don't want to go with Mom to buy it."

Bob nodded. "I can understand that." He stopped at the light on Skamania. "I suppose we could get one tomorrow. Or Sunday."

If we kept hitting the red lights, it would take us forever to get to Katherine's house. Lots of time to go back to Spurl and Manning and Travis. "Only don't tell Mom I asked you to buy it, okay? She said Liz and I aren't supposed to ask you to buy things."

Bob looked at me, then back at the road. "Your mother said that?"

I nodded. "It's Liz's fault. You know, all that stuff about

127

the cat costume. Mom said you're a walking wallet."

He raised his eyebrows. "She called me a walking wallet?" His voice had sharpened, the way it did sometimes at school. "A walking wallet," he repeated.

I felt a little jab of guilt. I hadn't actually meant to make him mad at Mom. "She said it in a nice way. I mean, I think she was joking."

He shook his head, and he didn't say anything else all the way to Katherine's.

I was hoping that she'd be standing outside, but she wasn't. I had to go up to the front door and ring the bell.

She opened the door right away, though, like she'd been waiting for me. She was wearing black jeans and a pink sweater. Her eyeshadow had pink glitter in it. I was glad to see she had on sneakers and not the boots.

"Hi," I said, and I wondered if I should have dressed up a little more.

"Hi," she said. "Cool T-shirt."

A man appeared behind her. He was wearing a brown suit. He had his tie loosened like he'd just gotten home from work. "This is my father," Katherine said. "David Chang." She said it like she'd rehearsed it.

"I'm glad to meet you, Jonah." Mr. Chang held out his hand. "I've heard a lot about you."

I hadn't heard anything about him. I took his hand and shook it. "I'm glad to meet you."

A woman who looked a lot like Katherine came through the kitchen doorway. She was carrying a little girl, about two or three. A little boy who looked like he was about Liz's age followed her. He stuck his tongue out at me.

"This is my mother, Sarah Chang. And my sister and brother." Katherine waved her hand at them like they didn't count.

Mrs. Chang smiled at me. "Hello, Jonah." She was wearing the kind of long, loose skirt and blouse that my mother called hippie clothes.

Mr. Chang was looking over my shoulder. "Is that Bob Decker out in the car? Sarah, I've been wanting to talk to him about that bond measure."

"Mother," Katherine said.

Mrs. Chang grabbed Mr. Chang, quick, by the sleeve. "Not now, David. Some other time." She looked at Katherine. "You have your money?"

Katherine rolled her eyes. "Of course."

"And you know where you're meeting the other kids?"

"Yes."

"And your dad will pick you and Jonah up at nine o'clock—"

"In front of the Made in Oregon store," Katherine finished. "You've told me a thousand times, Mom."

"I probably have." Mrs. Chang was still smiling. I was kind of surprised. My mother would have stopped a long time ago. "Well. Have a good time. It was nice meeting you, Jonah."

"You, too," I said, but Katherine was pulling me down the sidewalk by my arm.

Katherine climbed into the backseat. I wasn't sure if I should sit in the front or the back, but she moved way over to the middle, and then patted the seat beside her, so I climbed in.

Bob looked over the seat and smiled. "Hi, Katherine." She smiled back. "Hi, Mr. Decker." She sounded glad to see him.

Bob pulled away from the curb. He didn't say anything until he got to the stop sign. "The laser-tag place is in the little mall, right?"

"Right," I said.

He nodded. I was afraid he was going to keep on talking to us, but he leaned forward and clicked the radio on to the news show he liked to listen to. He adjusted the volume to the front of the car.

Katherine glanced at me. "Sorry about my mother."

"It's okay."

"And they made a big deal about my dad picking us up."

"It's okay," I said again.

She checked the back of Bob's head, then reached over and took my hand, on the seat, where Bob couldn't see. She smiled, and I smiled back. And I remembered this was my first date.

It was pretty quiet all the way to the mall. Bob pulled up to the main entrance. "Is this it?"

"Yeah," I said. "This is great." I half expected him to ask the same questions Mrs. Chang had asked, about money and meeting everybody, but he didn't.

"My dad will bring Jonah home," Katherine said as we climbed out of the car.

"Okay," Bob said. "Have fun."

"He's so cool," Katherine said. She moved close against my side.

"I guess," I said. I waited until he made the turn out of the parking lot. Then I put my arm around her shoulders.

We went into the mall. "We're supposed to meet them by the fountain," Katherine said. She was walking tight against my side. It sort of reminded me of a three-legged race, and her fuzzy sweater tickled my arm. Travis and Tiffany had always made it look so easy.

Amanda was already waiting in front of the fountain. Her mother was sitting on a bench near a potted plant. I stepped away from Katherine, but she kept hold of my hand. Mrs. Matzinger waggled her fingers at us. "Hi, Jonah. Hi, Katherine. Don't you look nice."

"She's not staying, is she?" Katherine whispered.

"No," Amanda said. She turned around and glared at her mother. "She's leaving in just a couple of minutes."

"I just want to make sure you all find each other," Mrs. Matzinger said.

Amanda groaned.

"Hi, guys." Kevin and Eric came around the back of the fountain. "Hi, Mrs. Matzinger." Kevin waved at her, and she waved back.

Amanda and Katherine were frowning at Eric. "I figured you wouldn't mind," Kevin said. "There's already a ton of people."

"Should we wait in the computer store?" Eric asked.

"No!" Amanda and Katherine said together.

"Hi!" Thuy and Jill came around the other side of the fountain. Emma and Sylvie were with them. Emma looked at me and looked away. My hand started to sweat inside Katherine's. "I figured you wouldn't mind if I asked Emma," Jill said. "And Sylvie's spending the night at Thuy's."

Katherine and Amanda looked at each other. Katherine let go of my hand and wiped hers on her pant leg.

"There's already a ton of kids," I said. And I smiled at Emma. But she was talking to Sylvie.

"It's kind of like a field trip," Eric said. He smiled around at all of us.

Katherine put her hands over her face. Emma and Sylvie were still whispering, their heads together. Emma's face was almost as red as her hair. I saw Thuy look at Jill, and they both shrugged.

"Well," Mrs. Matzinger said. "I guess everyone's here. Have a good time now." She walked off down the mall, her shoes making loud clacking noises on the tiles.

Nobody said anything for a couple of seconds. "Well, I'm starved," Kevin said finally. "Let's eat."

At the food court, everybody split up. I picked Mama Boffo's pizza because the line was the longest. By the time I got my food, Amanda and Thuy and Jill had pushed three tables together and had places for all of us to sit. "Katherine said you should sit there, Jonah," Amanda

133

said. "She'll be next to you when she gets back."

I sat down where she said. Eric and Kevin were in the middle, across from Jill and Thuy. Emma was at the far end of the table. She and Sylvie were sharing an order of fries. Amanda squished next to Kevin and me and took a bite of hamburger.

"You were a good Mercutio yesterday, Eric," Jill said. Eric slurped at his shake. "Thanks."

"Jonah's so lucky," Thuy said. "You don't have to worry about what part you get. Everybody knows you're going to be Romeo."

"Well, you never know." I picked a shriveled piece of pepperoni off my pizza. I wasn't feeling so hungry.

"I would love to be Juliet," Sylvie said.

"Not me," Amanda said. "I'd have to kiss Jonah." And Emma laughed, loud.

I reached over and tried to give Amanda a punch, but she ducked, and I hit my cup instead. Icy cold Coke spilled into my lap. I yelled and jumped up.

"Look who I found in the taco line." Katherine was standing behind me, holding a tray. Travis and Jerry were with her.

Travis grinned. "Well, I can tell Jonah is really excited to see us."

Gotcha!

I spent about twenty minutes in the bathroom, trying to get my pants dry. I used up all the paper towels, and I still had a big wet spot right in the front.

Katherine had gotten a guy to come with a mop and pail to clean up the spill. "It almost doesn't show," she whispered, as I sat down at the table. "I mean your pants."

"Right," I said.

Eric and Kevin were explaining laser-tag strategy to Amanda and Jill and Emma.

"The best team to be on is the red team," Kevin said.

"Because the yellow lights and the green lights look too much alike," Eric said. "If you're on the red team, you can just shoot everybody and gets lots of points."

"Do you want me to get you some napkins?" Katherine whispered.

"I'm okay."

"You get more points if you hit the Death Satellite," Thuy said.

"Yeah," Eric said, "but that's really hard."

"I know how to do it," Thuy said. Kevin and Eric looked at her. "I do," she said. "I play this a lot with my brother."

"Do you want me to get you another piece of pizza?" Katherine asked. "Your first one got all wet, and we—"

"I'm fine," I said. "It's okay. Never mind."

"Okay," Katherine said. She sounded sort of hurt.

Travis was perched on the end of the table. Jerry had squished in next to Sylvie. "Are you guys going to play laser-tag?" I asked.

Travis shrugged. "Sounds okay to me."

"I'll have to borrow some money," Jerry said.

"I'll lend you some," Sylvie said, and everybody laughed but Jerry.

As soon as everyone was done eating, we headed for the laser-tag place. Katherine walked over by Amanda and Kevin, like she was mad about something. I didn't care. I was too busy trying not to walk funny, because of my wet pants.

One of the employees, a woman in tight black jeans and

a tight black shirt that said, "Referee Rhonda," led us through a door into the "briefing room." It was a little room with three low, long steps facing a blank wall. "Just sit on one of the steps," Referee Rhonda said.

"If we're on the same step, we'll be on the same team," Eric said.

Amanda, Kevin, Eric, Jill, Katherine and I ended up on the first step. Emma and Sylvie and Thuy were on the step behind us, with Jerry and Travis. Emma ended up right behind me. I knew because I could smell her perfume.

Referee Rhonda went back into the waiting room and came back with a bunch of adults and two little kids who looked like they were Liz's age. She had the adults and one of the kids sit on the top step. "You'll be the green team." She sat the other little kid down next to Travis.

"Hey," Travis said, "we don't need any babies."

"Every team has to have six players," Referee Rhonda said. "You're the yellow team."

"Yes!" Eric said. "We're the red team!"

Referee Rhonda started explaining how the game worked. She talked about bases and markers and the Death Satellite and how you scored points. She sounded really bored. She sort of reminded me of Spurl. "No stalking," she said. "No covering up your target. No profanity."

"Damn," Travis said. Katherine reached back and hit him on the knee.

"Any questions?" Referee Rhonda looked at me, saw the wet spot and looked away. The adults started asking a whole bunch of dumb questions. Something tickled the back of my neck. I reached back, and my hand closed on Emma's knee. She pulled loose. I turned around to look at her, but she was turned toward Thuy.

When the adults finally ran out of questions, Referee Rhonda opened a door in the wall. "Okay. Come on into the vesting room."

There were racks of vests with the laser guns attached to them by wires that looked like telephone cords. I put my vest on. It was heavy and awkward.

Amanda looked down at the circle of red lights glowing on her chest. "I feel like a Christmas tree."

"Listen." Eric pulled all the red team into a little circle. "When it starts, Kevin and I are going to make an attack on the green base and try to take out their marker. Jonah and Amanda, you cover us. Jill and Katherine can provide backup."

Katherine was frowning. "I have no idea what you're

talking about, Eric." I smiled at her, to show her I was sorry, but she didn't smile back.

"Just shoot anything with a yellow or a green light," Kevin said.

Travis came over. His vest was glowing with little yellow lights. "Hey, girls. Want to see my gun?"

"You are so rude, Travis Hunter," Katherine said, and she grinned at him.

The adults finally all had their vests on. They were giggling and acting really dumb. "Okay," Referee Rhonda said. She opened another door behind us. "You're about to enter the mysterious and exciting world of Planet Laserdoom." She sighed and scratched her head. "If you have problems, look for me or Referee Richard. Watch your step."

The next room was probably about as big as the cafeteria at school, but it looked bigger, because it was so dark. The only lights were some dim yellow ones set around near the floor. Black shapes loomed around us, ramps and short walls and things that were probably supposed to be alien trees and rocks. Amanda clutched my arm and made me jump. "This is sort of spooky," she whispered.

"Yeah," I said. But at least nobody could see that my

pants were wet. I took my laser gun out of its holster. It was bigger than my arm and way heavier. I felt like Arnold Schwarzenegger in that movie with the robot.

Eric came up behind us. He pointed to the big ramp in the middle of the room. "That's how you get to the Death Satellite."

"Okay," Referee Rhonda said. "When you hear the buzzer, your time begins. When you hear it again, your time's up." She looked around at us. "Don't just stand there. Scatter!"

We scattered. Somehow I got mixed up into a clump of the adults, and by the time I managed to get free, everybody had disappeared.

The buzzer sounded. Somebody jumped out from behind a wall in front of me. A red light flared, and my vest buzzed. "Ha-ha! Got you, sucker!" It was the little kid on Travis's team. He took off before I could shoot him back.

I crouched down and sort of scuttled behind one of the rocks. Jerry was hiding there, next to one of the lights. He turned around, and I shot him right in the middle of his target.

"No fair. I wasn't ready," he said.

"Laser-tag isn't supposed to be fair, Jerry," I said. And I took off.

I shot five adults on my way across the room, and I got shot by the little kid again, by Thuy, and by somebody I suspected was Travis.

Amanda was hiding behind a wall near the exit door. I recognized her by her laugh. "I'm out of ammo," she said.

"Already?" I checked my gun. Lights glowed all the way along the barrel.

"I've been following those adults around and shooting them. They're so clueless." She peeked around the wall, then jumped back. "Quick. There's one now."

She shoved me out, and I shot wildly at a dark figure scurrying past. His vest buzzed and hummed, and he swore.

"No profanity," Referee Richard shouted from a corner. I ducked back behind the wall.

"See," Amanda said. "Wasn't that great?"

I laughed. "You're really getting into this."

"It's way more fun than I expected." She rose up to a crouch. "I have to go find a re-arming station."

"Do you know where Katherine is?" I asked. I was feeling sort of bad about being mean to her back at the food court. This was her big date thing, after all.

"She may be backing Kevin up at the green base," Amanda said. She was gone again before I could ask her where the green base was.

I couldn't really believe that Katherine was backing anybody up at any base, but then again, I never would have believed that Amanda would be so into this. Somebody ran around the corner and shot me.

I stood up. A base marker was flashing across a nearby wall. I dashed across the open space, ducked behind a tree thing, crawled behind a low wall and started shooting at the marker. I could tell when I hit it because it would stop flashing for a few seconds and hum.

Eric came up behind me. "This is the red base, dummy. You don't shoot at your own base!"

"Jeez, Jonah." Kevin was behind him. They stood back to back, guarding each other.

"Sorry," I said. "How was I supposed to know?"

Eric pointed his gun at a big sign on the wall. It said, "Red Base."

Sylvie and Jerry popped up from behind the wall and started shooting at our light. Kevin and Eric drove them off with a lot of shooting and yelling.

"Have you seen Katherine?" I shouted to Sylvie as she ran off, but she didn't answer me.

"I think she's over by the green base," Kevin said.

Two adults popped up and started shooting, and Kevin and Eric started shooting back.

I found the yellow base, but Katherine wasn't there. I checked behind all the tree shapes and behind the walls. I got shot about twenty times, but I managed to shoot Sylvie and Jerry and a bunch of the adults. The little kids were too fast.

I was chasing one of them when I came around one of the low walls and tripped over somebody huddled in the dark. "Sorry," I said.

"My fault," Emma said.

I stopped and knelt down next to her. "I didn't hurt you, did I?" I could barely see her face in the darkness.

"No," she said. "I'm okay." She sighed. "That little kid? The one on the adult team? He keeps following me around and shooting me."

"He's stalking you," I said. "Do you want me to go find one of the referees? It's against the rules. Stalking, I mean. They'll make him quit."

"No. You don't have to find a referee." She wiggled

143

around a little. "I'm sorry about that thing with the dress-ing container, by the way. I didn't mean to get you into trouble."

"It's okay," I said. I cleared my throat. I wanted to tell her I really liked her. I wanted to ask her if there was any way we could still be friends.

Kevin ran around the corner. "Jonah! We need you to help attack the Death Satellite." He saw Emma. "Hey. You're not on our team!" And he shot her.

"Kevin," I started, but Emma was crawling away around the corner. "Come *on,* Jonah," Kevin said. I got up and followed him. Three of the adults ran past us, with Sylvie and Jerry and Thuy right behind them. Jerry took a shot at me, but he missed. Thuy got me.

Jill and Amanda and Eric were hiding at the foot of the ramp. Eric pointed at me. "Jonah. You stay here and guard the way up."

"Fine," I said. They all swarmed up the ramp, and I crouched down next to the wall.

"Hey."

I turned around, and the little kid from the yellow team shot me. "Gotcha!" he shouted. Then he put his finger on his lips. "Somebody's under there," he whispered.

I looked through the crisscross panels that covered the

underside of the ramp. He was right. Two people *were* under there, standing very close together. I could tell, even in the dim light, that they were kissing.

The kid ducked through the opening in the panels. "No hiding your targets," he said. "That's cheating."

The two people stepped apart. One of them was wearing a yellow vest. "Oh," the kid said. "You're on my team." I knew it had to be Travis.

The other person had on a red vest. "Gotcha!" the kid yelled. And he shot Katherine right in the middle of her target.

Sort of a Weird Date

I took a step back from the paneling. Katherine and Travis were looking at the little kid. I didn't think they'd seen me.

The buzzer sounded. "Time's up!" Referee Rhonda shouted. She started herding people toward the door.

I followed Jerry and Sylvie into the vesting room. "That was so cool," Jerry said. "I got like a billion points."

"A billion. I'm sure," Sylvie said. But she was smiling, and it didn't sound mean.

Jerry grinned and, when Sylvie turned away, he whispered, "I am hot tonight."

"That's great, Jer," I said, and I hung up my vest and gun.

Thuy and Kevin and Eric came in. They were talking

about the Death Satellite. Katherine walked in behind them. She looked at me, then looked away.

Amanda, Emma, and Jill came in with the adults. Travis was last. He was bugging the two little kids, pulling on their vests, and shoving them against each other.

"Big jerk," one of them said, and he kicked Travis hard in the shin.

"Way to go, little kid," I said.

Katherine frowned at me, but Travis grinned. He came over and punched me in the arm. "Some fun, huh, Jonah?"

"Tons of fun," I said, and I punched him back, harder.

He looked surprised, and I braced myself to take his next hit. But Amanda grabbed my arm. "Come on," she said. "Eric says they're printing out the score sheets."

The computer was just printing out our scores. Our team had the most points. Amanda had the highest score of all. "Yes!" she said and pumped her fist in the air.

"Rambo, meet Amandabo," Eric said.

"Wambo," Travis said, and he laughed.

Katherine giggled, and I saw Amanda frown at her.

Sylvie and Emma and Jerry came over. Jerry and Sylvie were bumping shoulders, shoving each other back and forth. Jerry had his arm around Sylvie's shoulder. I wanted to ask Emma how she had done, but I was too mad to talk

to anybody. I wanted to ask Katherine what had been going on, but I didn't know if I wanted to know.

Travis came up on the other side of Amanda. "Hey,
Trav," Jerry said, "how'd you do?" I didn't think he really
cared. He just wanted Travis to see him with Sylvie.

Travis shrugged. "I think there was something wrong
with my gun. I didn't get a lot of shots off."

"Well," Katherine said loudly. She clapped her hands,
like Ms. Landau. "It was fun. Wasn't it?" She was blushing.

"Are we playing again?" Thuy asked.

"That's the plan," Kevin said. "Isn't it?" He looked at
Amanda, and she nodded. "We have to wait, though," she
said. "There's a game going on now, and we play after it."

Eric pulled on Kevin's arm. "Let's play *Incredible Car-
nage.*"

"Oh, I got on the high scores last week," Thuy said. Eric
and Kevin followed her over to the big bank of video
games running along one wall.

Travis and Jerry started dropping quarters into the air
hockey table in the corner. Sylvie and Emma and Jill
leaned on the table to watch. "I play the loser," Emma
said.

"You mean the winner," Jill said.

"I don't want to play the winner," Emma said, and they

148

all laughed. For some reason, watching them made me feel even worse.

"What do you think, Jonah?" Amanda asked.

"About what?"

"About where to go afterwards?" Amanda said. "We'll have some time left. Starbucks or Baskin-Robbins?"

Travis scored a goal. He shouted and raised his hands up above his head. He looked at Katherine, and she laughed. And then she saw me looking at her, and she stopped.

I knew I had to get out of there. "I'm really not feeling so good. I really sort of have a headache." As soon as I said it, I realized it was true. "A bad headache," I added.

Amanda frowned at me. Katherine said, "You do look kind of . . . not so good."

"Yeah. Well. I was thinking maybe I should just head home."

"What?" Amanda looked at me like I was nuts. "Are you nuts?"

I waited for Katherine to say, "Oh, poor Jonah." I waited for her to say, "Don't go, Jonah. It'll be more fun if you stay."

But she said, "Can you get a ride home?"

"I think so."

"Because my dad's not coming until nine, you know. And that's an awful long time for you to just sit here and wait, if you're feeling sick."

"I'm pretty sure Bob can come get me," I said.

She gave me a big, cheery smile. "Then it's all settled." She walked over to the air-hockey table. "Jonah's sick. He's going home."

Amanda nudged me with her elbow. "Why don't you stay? It'll be more fun if you stay."

"Not for me," I said.

"Now we'll have to reorganize the teams," Thuy said. And they all started arguing about that. I thought maybe Emma would look over at me. Look sad or worried or something. But she didn't.

I went over to the pay phone and called home. The phone rang about five times, and I was starting to think that maybe Bob and Liz had gone somewhere, and I was starting to think maybe I should just stay, maybe it was dumb to leave, when Bob answered. I asked him to come get me, and he said, "Sure."

"You don't have to," I said. "If it's a problem."

"No problem," he said.

When I hung up, Katherine was standing beside me. "I

really hope you feel better, Jonah," she said.

"Yeah. Well," I said.

She rocked back and forth on her heels. It made her sweater move up and down, and you could see her belly button. "This has been sort of a weird date. I mean, it hasn't turned out exactly the way I thought."

"No kidding," I said. "I gotta go." And I went to wait outside.

Bob showed up in about ten minutes. Liz was with him. I climbed into the backseat of the car. Liz turned around from the front. She was wearing a black cat costume. The tail was long enough to flip back over the seat. She grinned. "It's even got claws," she said, and she held up her hands to show me.

I looked at Bob. He shook his head. "It wasn't me."

"Maureen sent it," Liz said, "Federal Express!" She pointed a claw at me. "And I didn't beg for it or anything. I just told Daddy when he called that I wanted to be a cat for Halloween."

I knew Mom was still going to be pissed.

When we got home, I went straight up to my room and lay down on my bed. I stared up at the ceiling in the light from the hall. I could hear Liz and Bob downstairs and the rattle of the popcorn maker. I could hear Liz's high-pitched whiny voice and Bob's low, quiet rumble. I wondered if they were talking about me.

I wondered if they were talking about me back at the laser-tag place, too. I should have stayed so they couldn't talk about me. I should have stayed so I'd know for sure what was going on. So I'd know if Travis and Katherine were still under that ramp, kissing.

I wondered if anybody else had seen them. Maybe Kevin or Thuy or Sylvie. I groaned. Sylvie was the rumor queen. If she knew, then by Monday morning everybody in the entire eighth grade would know that Katherine had dumped me for Travis Hunter.

How could she do that to me? How could she be kissing Travis, when I'd never even kissed her? Not even when we'd rehearsed the skit in drama. And now she'd probably been kissing Travis ever since I'd left. I reminded myself I didn't even like her that much. I reminded myself that now I could go out with Emma. Only Emma didn't want to go out with me.

I grabbed my hair in both hands and yelled, "Aaaagh!

"Jonah?" Mom was standing in the open doorway. "Are you all right?"

I let go of my hair. "I don't feel so good."

152

"That's what Bob said." She came in, clicked on my desk lamp, and sat down on the bed beside me. "Where do you hurt?"

"All over."

She rested her hand against my forehead. Her hand felt soft and cool. Maybe I really was sick. Maybe I had a fever, and I'd have to stay home from school for the whole week. Or even longer. Maybe I was dying, and then Travis and Katherine would be sorry. And Emma, too.

Mom took her hand away. "You don't feel warm. Maybe it was something you ate."

I realized I hadn't eaten *anything.* "I don't think so," I said.

"How was laser-tag? Did you have fun? I mean, before you felt sick?"

"It was okay." I closed my eyes. "I think it gave me a headache. There's flashing lights, and it's hard to see, and people are yelling." I opened my eyes.

She was smiling. "Was everybody there?"

"A whole bunch of people," I said. Way more than needed to be there.

"Mom!" Liz shrieked. "The movie's starting!"

"I'm with Jonah!" Mom shouted back. "I'll be there soon." She sat up straighter and folded her hands into her

153

lap. She sighed. "Bob said he's been hearing some things at school . . ."

"We talked about it already." I wiggled up a little on the pillow, so I was sitting up straighter.

"Oh." She looked surprised. "When?"

"In the car."

"Oh," she said again. "So. It's not going to be a problem?"

"It's not going to be a problem," I said, and my voice cracked, the way it does when I'm upset or annoyed.

She smiled and patted my knee. "Don't be mad at Bob, Jonah. The poor guy doesn't know if he's fish or fowl."

For a second, all I could think about was Travis's stepfather who was crazy. "He thinks he's a fish?"

"It's a saying. I mean he's trying to figure out where he fits in."

It sort of depressed me, to think you could be as old as Bob, really old, and still not feel like you fit in. It sounded like eighth grade forever.

Mom smoothed the bedspread next to me. "It must be like this at your dad's house, too," she said. "Everybody trying to sort out where they belong."

I could tell she really wanted me to say yes. "Yeah," I said. "It's like that." Although it wasn't really. Dad was still pretty much Dad, making dumb jokes and yelling about how much TV we watched. And Maureen obviously just wanted us to like her and the baby. "Did you see the cat costume?" I asked.

"Yes. I saw the cat costume." Mom rubbed the bridge of her nose. "Sometimes I feel like there are a few too many adults in this family."

"Yeah," I said again. "Me, too." I sat up totally straight. "By the way, I asked Bob to buy me a jockstrap."

She blinked. "Well. That's fine."

"I need it for this thing in drama." I waved my hand. "It's a long story. But I didn't want you to think I was asking for stuff. You know."

"No. No. I'm glad you asked him." She smiled. "I wouldn't even know for sure where to buy one." She stood up. "Why don't you come downstairs and watch the movie with us? Have some popcorn."

I thought about it. "I think I'll stay up here."

She put her hand on my hair. "Do you feel better?"

Not really, I thought. "A little," I said.

It Just Sort of Happened

All day Saturday, I kept thinking Katherine would call me. Or maybe even Travis. But nobody did.

Liz went to Stephanie's on Sunday afternoon to show her the cat costume. Mom and Bob went to Doug and Diane's to babysit. I was sitting in the living room playing Fog Quest when the doorbell rang. It was Amanda.

It was raining hard, and even just running over from her house, she'd gotten soaked. She shook her head, and drops of water sprayed out, kind of like a wet dog. I stepped back. "Come on in."

We went into the living room. She sat in the armchair. "I don't want to wreck your couch," she said. She shoved at her bangs, and they were so wet they stood straight up from her forehead. It made her look like a little kid. "I just got the weirdest phone call from Thuy."

I sat down on the couch. "What did she say?"

"I guess Sylvie's calling people and telling them that Travis and Katherine were kissing at the laser-tag place."

The rumor queen. "Under the ramp," I said.

Amanda bugged her eyes. "Sylvie called you, too?"

"No. I saw them myself."

"You're kidding." She sat back in the chair and crossed her legs. "You're kidding," she said again. Suddenly she snapped her fingers. "*That's* why you left early. You weren't really sick at all."

Amanda Matzinger, Girl Detective, I thought. "That's why," I said. Amanda looked really shocked and horrified. It made me feel sort of good. I wanted her to feel bad. "And you said it was going to be just perfect," I said.

"What do you mean?"

"Katherine and me. You said it was perfect. You said Katherine liked me a lot. A whole lot."

"She did like you. I mean, she does like you." Water was trickling down the sides of her face, and she wiped it away. "It's not like this is my fault or anything, Jonah."

I snorted. "I would have been fine without you messing around." If Amanda hadn't started meddling, I would be going out with Emma by now. It made me feel sad, thinking about Emma.

Amanda leaned forward. "You thanked me, Jonah Truman. You thanked me for getting you guys together."

"Look, Amanda. You're supposed to be feeling sorry for me, not yelling at me."

She laughed. Then she sighed. "I can't believe they were kissing out there in front of everybody. It is just incredibly tacky."

"No kidding," I said. Although I would have kissed Emma. If she would have kissed me.

"And Travis Hunter." Amanda stuck her tongue out really far. It was purple. "I thought you and Travis were sort of friends."

"Yeah. So did I." I picked at something sticky on the knee of my jeans. "Your tongue's all purple," I said.

"I was eating a Popsicle when Thuy called." Amanda shook her head again. "Katherine Chang and Travis Hunter. It's like Marcia Brady and . . . and Beavis."

I laughed. Amanda was really funny. If only she wasn't going out with Kevin. Except going out with Amanda would be like going out with my own sister. And I was never going out with anybody ever again. All of a sudden, I knew it was true. "I'm never going out with anybody ever again," I said.

Amanda raised her eyebrows, but she didn't say anything. She shoved my leg. "I was talking to Kevin, and he thought maybe we could go see the new Halloween Massacre movie. You and me and him."

"What about Eric?"

"He doesn't like horror movies."

I knew they were just being nice to me, but I wanted them to be nice to me. "That would be okay. Tell Kevin it's okay with me."

"And he said I should tell you that you did really great at laser-tag."

"Yeah. Well, tell him I thought he was pretty good, too."

She nodded. "And I'll tell him you like his hair and the outfit he was wearing on Friday."

Kevin had been wearing jeans and a Dilbert T-shirt. "What?" I said. And then I saw the way she was grinning, and I got it. "Yeah, right," I said. "Tell him that, too."

I got to school early on Monday morning. I figured it was worse to have people talking about me when I wasn't there than when I was there.

I stopped by my locker and dropped off my backpack and the jockstrap I'd painted gold the day before. I stood there for a second, just staring into my locker. It still smelled like the banana I'd had in my lunch the Tuesday before. I took a deep breath, anyway, to brace myself, and slammed the door shut.

Katherine was standing behind the open door.

It was just like in one of those scary movies, where it turns out the crazed murderer has been hiding behind the door all along. I jumped five feet and just managed to keep myself from screaming.

Katherine jumped, too. But she didn't stab me or shoot me or anything like that. She just handed me a note. "Here. I was going to put it in your locker, but . . . well . . ." She blushed.

I was really regretting I'd gotten to school early. Why hadn't I been late? Why hadn't I convinced Mom to let me stay home sick? I unfolded the note. "Dear Jonah. I'm really sorry things didn't work out. I hope you understand and that we'll always be friends. I think you're a really, really nice guy." She hadn't signed it.

I wanted to wad it up and toss it way up on top of the lockers. But I didn't.

She was watching the toe of her boot make lines on the carpeting. "It just sort of happened," she said. "It was really weird."

I nodded. I could understand *that*.

"I hope you don't totally hate me."

"I don't totally hate you," I said. But I really don't like you much, I thought.

"Well." She sort of waved her hand. "I've gotta go." And she walked off down the hall.

I leaned against my locker. So that was that. I'd officially been dumped by Katherine Chang. I looked at the note. "We'll always be friends." I snorted and wadded the note up and tossed it on top of the lockers.

"Jonah." Bob came up behind me. For a second, I thought he was going to say something about throwing garbage, but he didn't. He handed me a piece of paper. "Ron Spurl dropped this by my office. He thought you might be interested. He said his sons play in the league."

I looked at the paper. There was a picture of a guy in full hockey gear at the top, followed by a bunch of information and an application form.

"It's a roller-hockey league," Bob said.

I turned the paper over. There was nothing on the back. "Mr. Spurl has kids?"

Bob nodded. "But it's not like you'd be on the same

team or anything." He tapped the paper. "It sounds like maybe a good way to get to play, learn some skills. Now that you're not going to be playing at the school . . ." His voice trailed off.

I knew he and Mom must have talked about me and Travis. I thought about Melanie's fat stepfather and Travis's crazy stepfather. And I remembered that being old must suck just as much as eighth grade. "I'll think about it," I said.

"Great," he said. He smiled this big, happy smile, and I told myself it probably wouldn't be a dorky skating rink with a bunch of dorky little Spurls.

I folded the flyer and put it in my pocket. "By the way," I said, "you might want to make the popcorn without cheese. Just once in a while."

"What?" Bob frowned.

"Liz hates cheese on popcorn."

"Oh," he said. Then he said, "Oh," again, like it suddenly made sense. He smiled at me. "Thanks, Jonah."

I shrugged. "No problem."

He went off down the hall. I leaned back against my locker. All the teachers were apparently talking about me and Travis. All the kids would be talking about me and

Katherine. Walt Morey Middle School really needed to get a life.

By the time lunch was over, I'd seen Travis and Katherine together three times. I figured everybody else had seen them, too. And I figured that the worst was over. But I'd forgotten about drama club.

Ms. Landau clapped her hands. "Let's get started, folks." She was wearing big baggy checked pants with suspenders, like a clown. "We've got the skits to do today, and then we're going to talk about the cast list." She looked at her clipboard. "Rumpelstiltskin will go first."

We were actually doing the skits up on the stage in the cafeteria. Amanda sat down beside me. "Did you bring the jockstrap?"

I nodded. I was watching Katherine and Travis. They were sitting at a table in the back. Travis had his arm around her.

Melanie sat down on the other side of me. "Did you bring the jockstrap?"

"Yes!" I shouted, and Ms. Landau frowned and said, "Shh!"

Our group went last. It was dark backstage, and Cathy and Amanda got their costumes mixed up, and then Travis couldn't find his godfather hat and gun. Melanie kept whispering, "Hurry up! Hurry up!" really loudly.

"Whenever you're ready," Ms. Landau shouted from the cafeteria.

It went okay, in the beginning. We all remembered our lines and where we should be standing, more or less. The other kids laughed when they were supposed to. And after Travis told me he had an offer I couldn't refuse, and I went off and came back on wearing the golden jockstrap, I thought they'd never stop laughing. Ms. Landau laughed so hard, she nearly fell off the table.

The worst part was the very end. The Princess came to Cinderelvis's house. The jockstrap didn't fit my stepbrothers, although Amanda and Cathy tried really hard to get it on. The kids in the audience laughed so much, we had to stop. And then Katherine came over to me with the jockstrap. And everybody got very quiet, the audience and Cathy and Amanda and Melanie and everybody. Somebody in front whispered, "They broke up, you know." And somebody in the back said, "Travis and Katherine. Didn't you know?" I hadn't realized people on stage could hear the audience so well.

I could tell Katherine could hear them, too, because she blushed.

I took the jockstrap and wiggled into it over my jeans. "It fits," Katherine said, and Ms. Landau was the only one laughing, because everybody knew now Katherine and I were supposed to kiss. It had made sense a week ago. A week ago, I'd been thinking it was going to be the best part of the whole play.

Katherine was just standing there, staring at me, like she couldn't move. I knew Travis was watching us from backstage. Somebody in the audience said something, and somebody else laughed. And then Emma said, "It's just a play, for gosh sakes. It's just *acting.*"

And I stepped across the space, and I kissed Katherine, real quick, right on the lips. For the first time and the last. And then it was over.

When we were out of our costumes, Ms. Landau had us sit down with the other kids at the cafeteria tables. Amanda made room for me next to her and Kevin. Emma and Sylvie were sitting at the table behind us.

Ms. Landau started reading out the cast list for *Romeo and Juliet.* I kind of liked that she just did it, without explaining or apologizing or anything.

When she was done, everybody just sat there.

"I'm Juliet?" Katherine said finally.

"And Eric's Romeo?" Sylvie said.

165

Eric looked like somebody'd just told him there was no such thing as alien abductions.

Amanda and Kevin looked at me. "Way to go, Eric," I said.

And then everybody was talking and laughing or complaining all at once. Amanda and Kevin went over to talk to Eric. People started milling around. A bunch stood around Ms. Landau.

Emma leaned over and put a hand on my shoulder. Sylvie was over talking to Thuy and Jill. "I'm really sorry, Jonah," Emma said.

I wasn't sure if she meant about Romeo or about Katherine. "It's okay," I said. And it was. "Mercutio gets to swordfight, and he gets to die."

"And he doesn't kiss Juliet," Emma said.

"Thank goodness," I said, and we both laughed.

Emma leaned closer to me. "I have a really important question to ask you."

"What's that?" I grinned. I was waiting for smelly feet or smiley Smurfs.

"Do you want to go to the football game on Friday night with me?" She put up her hand. "It's homecoming, and lots of people will be there. My parents can drive us, because they go, too, but we don't have to sit with them." She frowned. "It's not a date or anything."

"Of course not," I said. I nodded. "I'd like to go. It sounds like fun."

She grinned. She had a great grin. "Okay. Check with your mom and call me, or tell me tomorrow."

"I'll call you," I said.

"Do you have my phone number?"

"Oh, no."

She pulled a purple felt pen out of her pocket and wrote her phone number on the back of my hand. She wrote "Emma" underneath. Then she stood up. "I have to go ask Ms. Landau what the nurse's costume looks like."

Across the room I heard Travis say, "We have a science test on Thursday?"

And Katherine said, "Don't worry. I'll remind you."

Amanda sat down where Emma had been. "I can just imagine what the friar wears," she said. She looked at me. "What did Emma want?"

I shrugged. "We're going to the football game at the high school on Friday."

Amanda raised her eyebrows. "No kidding. I thought you were never going to go out with anybody ever again."

"It's just a football game, Amanda."

"Right. And Emma's nice."

"She's very nice. And she's funny." I thought about it for minute. "And she draws great pictures of Mrs. Hassel."

Amanda laughed. "Well. There you go." She nudged me with her shoulder. "I told you so."

"Told me what?"

"I told you drama club would be good for you."

"Yeah," I said. "It's not as bad as I thought."

I'd forgotten my math book, and I had to stop by my locker when drama club was over. A note was lying on top of my science book. It said JONAH TRUMAN on the outside. It wasn't from Katherine. Or Emma. I opened it up.